MW01138271

The
Ghosts of Melrose

a novel
by

Buzz Malone

Dedications

This book is dedicated to Lorri, the love of my life. Without her support and guidance throughout the entire process I'd still be only talking about the story instead of you being able to read it. She is my toughest critic, my strongest ally, and my best friend. Also, she is the amazing photographer who created the cover art for this book. Thank you!

I'd also be remiss if I did not thank my father who continuously harped on me to write a book. Both of my parents have always been incredibly supportive of each and every one of my life's zany adventures. Thank you, Mom and Dad, for never giving up on me.

Thank you to the people of Melrose, Iowa too. All throughout my childhood, Melrose and the characters who once filled her streets were the subject of a thousand incredible stories. Even now when I visit I can almost see them walking the street and hear them in a thick Irish brogue, welcoming me. More than anyone, this book is for them, the real Ghosts of Melrose.

And finally, a very special thank you to my dear friends Banjo and Martha whose love and whose story inspired this novel.

Chapter 1   The Road to Nowhere

Set among the rolling hills of Southern Iowa, Melrose is but the leftover remnants of a place that used to be. It is not a destination, but rather, a brief distraction for the campers and boaters and fishermen on their way to Lake Rathbun. Were it not for the construction of the lake in the nineteen-seventies, what precious little that remains of Melrose may have disappeared entirely.

Weekend water lovers turn south off of U.S. Highway 34 and pass over the large hills. Children wave their hands through the air out the windows like airplanes coasting through the wind. Happy families in trucks and SUVs, heavily laden with supplies and tents and campers and boats, slow for their descent into the steep Melrose bottom. As they slow, they see the homemade plywood sign with a leprechaun welcoming them to Melrose, "Iowa's Little Ireland."

For those souls who pass through for their first time, many look at the old buildings for an antique shop, a museum, a bar, or even a gas station. But nothing remains. The shops and buildings that once were the heart of a bustling community are now only facades, adorned with the names of businesses and owners that exist only in the stories of residents long passed.

As the weekend families pass, they realize that it is only a bump in the road, a brief pause in their journey and nothing more. To most, Melrose is only that; an inconvenience on their way to somewhere else. A steep hill, a sharp corner, cross the railroad tracks and leave Melrose behind you like the rest of the world apparently has. To the passing families, there is nothing to give them further pause. It is but a dying remnant of a place that offers nothing, and appears to have never been.

As the children with their airplane hands out the windows pass, the sound of their laughter fills the still air of the Melrose bottom. In the empty shadows, the ghosts of Melrose smile knowingly and remember a time when the streets were bustling and alive. They hear their own children laughing and running along the decked walkways that lined the businesses. They see the beat cop walking down the road toward one of a dozen bars and taverns. They hear the clickety clack of horse hooves and the rattling of wagon wheels. They hear the rumbling of cars downshifting to pass draft horses and the roar of their engines as they power through the boggy mud road. Almost nothing remains in Melrose today, but to them, to the ghosts of Melrose, it is everything.

Chapter 2   In the Beginning

August, 1847

The early morning sun shone brightly into the clearing where the short, stout man led his team of draft horses. High above his head, he could see the leaves trembling to the tune of a light breeze, but no hint of the wind penetrated the hills and the thick foliage to relieve his sweating brow. It was before noon still and the humidity found his eyes filled with sweat as he hooked onto another oak log.

Below him was a small creek that flowed with fresh water from its mouth just a few miles to the west. Above him, the foundation of what would become his home and a small store took shape in the clearing left behind by the natives. Only a few years prior they had abandoned this small clearing, having been pushed to the west by the latest treaty.

Some native families remained in the north part of the county, but most simply packed up and moved along, making way for men like John Drew to fill in the voids behind them. Back in Illinois and points further east, they talked of the frontier and of the wilderness and the wild places. Adventurous souls like John Drew sought their fortunes in this "wilderness" by following well worn trails and building upon the cleared lands that had served as gardens for hundreds of years before they were born.

Drew had not simply chosen a random spot on a map though. He was no gambling adventurer, but rather, a well established business owner from back east. His site was carefully selected along the future route of the C.B. & Q. Railway. Everyone knew the route and hundreds speculated their futures along it, hoping to strike it rich and become founding father to the next Chicago or St. Louis of the west. But Drew knew more than the route. The husband of his own sister was the construction planning engineer for the C.B. & Q. and Drew's site would be one of the many construction hubs along the way where men and material would eventually amass.

It would be ten more years before the engineers and earth moving crews made their way to what would later become Melrose. Drew's spot though, was only a mile from one of the major east to west wagon trails. The trail (known then as the Mormon Trace), would eventually become US Hwy 34. His site was already a well used stopping point. The main trailhead diverted to an opening along the spring fed creek where the water flowed both fresh and clean and weary travelers could fill their water barrels and rest in the clearing.

Over the course of the next decade, Drew finished his store with sleeping quarters in the rear. Later, he added outbuildings to serve as both inn and smith shop. As time passed, entrepreneurial neighbors filled in the void expanses of land around him. With the commerce came a slow but steady growth and by 1855 a small community existed of a few dozen souls. On a nearby hill they even erected a small Methodist church.

As the railroad approached, they built at a feverish pace, inns and a breakfast and another store and even a few speculative homes and buildings to be sold to late arriving entrepreneurs. By the time the railroad crews were set to descend upon them, they stood ready and poised to become wealthy. The merchants were ready as any could have been, but nothing could have prepared them for what was to come.

There were some two dozen Methodists living in the quiet and peaceful bottom when the railroad advance engineers arrived to perform their final surveys. Despite every attempt by the surveyors to warn the merchants of what lie in their own wake, they were politely dismissed by the men who dreamed of the wealth that was sure to arrive with the railroad crews.

"It will be as a great flood of men into this bottom. A plague unfit for any Christians to live amongst. Just as likely to wipe you and yours from the face of the earth as the great flood of Noah," warned a surveyor to Drew.

Drew had only smiled unwittingly, believing the words to merely be an attempt by the railroad itself to buy him out of the fortune that he had planned and worked for over the past decade. A man like Drew would be neither cajoled nor frightened from what was rightfully his own. He'd sown the seeds and, by God, he'd reap what was rightfully his.

Chapter 3   A Great Pestilence

The township proper, as had been the almost devious plan from its humble beginning, sat adjacent to property owned by the C.B. & Q. Railway Company. Overnight, the area was flooded with men. Hundreds of Irishmen poured into the bottom each day.

One merchant, gone on business for only two weeks to Chicago, was stunned at what he discovered upon his return. Entire expanses of timber had been felled along the creek bottom and stables lodging scores of draft horses and oxen had been erected in his absence. Surrounding the stables was a tent camp of the likes and proportion only seen before during mass troop movements of the United States Army itself, and then only during times of war.

At first, there indeed were tremendous profits made by the local merchants. In only a few weeks time however, the C.B. & Q. merchants had arrived. Having paid the C.B. & Q. for the privilege to establish their shops on railroad property, the new Irish merchants quickly monopolized the local trade. The railroad itself intervened and soon only the new merchants were allowed to establish lines of credit that could be obtained against a railroad man's wages. Payment was guaranteed by the railroad itself. The local merchants had no such agreement with the railroad and therefore no guarantee of payment on lines of credit. To compete they issued their own lines of credit at better terms and the Irish quickly used it to obtain all the goods they could carry.

With the traveling company store came the traveling private goons. Pinkertons and other agencies served the purpose of law enforcement for hire. Beyond the scope of working for the railroads to protect property and thwart efforts made at unionizing the rail workers, the agencies also received a cut of the hefty profits from the traveling merchants. At first, their fee was used only to protect the property of the merchants themselves. But as time progressed, the agencies also worked to ensure that no railroad men were purchasing any goods from anyone else. When local merchants lowered their prices further to draw away clientele, the same Pinkerton goons were paid to squash the competition altogether.

So it was that the great fire swept through the town in 1866, burning homes and businesses alike. John Drew had built the town with his own hands. He had carved the thing out of timber felled with his own axe. He had made his home, built a church, and constructed a town in anticipation of the railroad.

Within less than a year, the Irish had bought all of his goods and then bought the replenished stock on credit; credit they had failed to repay under the sanctioned protection of hired goons. What had not ruined him from the run on store credit had been stolen by the roving bands of Irishmen who, each night, haunted the every dark corner of the valley for miles around.

Nothing was safe from them but the railroad's own property and that of the merchants who served their men. When the railroad did come up missing items one night, three Irishmen were taken from among the ranks at random and shot in the head by Pinkerton agents. And so, but for the rare occurrence, the railroad's property was left untouched. No one else however, would be safe from the great pestilence of poor working men.

Within weeks of the arrival of the Irish came hundreds of dirty women and children. Taverns sprang up in their wake like popped corn and brothels first run from the backs of wagons were moved into tents and then into makeshift lean-tos. By the time John Drew had found his property burned to the ground, the Irish brothels and shanty taverns alone outnumbered the town's original inhabitants by five to one.

Hope and anticipation by the locals had been dispelled by the constant fear of being surrounded by men who had little or nothing to lose. Many of them spoke no English and all of them were dirty and had a hungry look about their bodies and an even hungrier look upon their eyes. The sounds of drunken screaming and men being beaten filled the night air of the bottom. The local merchants and their families could only lay awake listening to it all and waiting with guns in hand for the sounds to grow too near.

John Drew knew no such fear. He had come to the bottom, to Iowa, not only seeking entrepreneurial riches, but to leave what had remained of his old life behind him. The store he had left abandoned back home and his own first house, he had burned to the ground himself after the illness had come. His own wife and three children, all, had succumbed to the disease, and only he had remained. So very much like the Irishmen, he too had nothing to lose but his life and fear of death was not left in him.

No. Drew would not be pushed along out of what he himself had created. Only two days after the charred ashes of his buildings had ceased to smolder, he began to rebuild. Neither Pinkertons, nor any pestilence of Irishmen could force him from it. In the end, no one would try to make him go. As he stood upon the rungs of a make-shift ladder driving home a wood peg into the framing of his new building, two Pinkerton men approached him from behind. It was shortly after noon in the light of day when he turned to see who was about and the rifles blasted away. John Drew, founding father of what would come to be known as Melrose, lay dead amongst his store's ashes with his blood pooled around him.

In the weeks that followed, an Irish railroader (and known union sympathizer) would be arrested by Pinkerton agents and found guilty of the murder of John Drew by a Railroad appointed judge. The Irishman was shortly thereafter hanged for his alleged crime. The railroad would observe the occasion by granting everyone an unheard of day of rest from construction activities so that all could see what became of trade unionists in this country.

11

Nineteen years after John Drew had laid claim to the ground in the vacant bottom and only two years after the arrival of the railroad and the newly immigrated Irish, a small group of merchant Irishmen plotted out a town of their own. It was 1866, and the plat which they surveyed growing up the hill from the rail yards and to the north of the tracks sprawling out in either direction, was given the Irish name of Melrose. In 1867, the Irishmen began to petition the Catholic Church to provide them with a priest.

It would be over 100 years before anyone ran a business in Melrose whose name was not Murphy or Sullivan or O'Neal or the like. Few who were not Catholic AND Irish both, dared to so much as step foot in the street of the town that had been founded upon so much blood and whose citizens kept the pools flowing fresh.

Chapter 4   Deliverance from Evil

In 1870, the Holy Roman Catholic Church heard the pleas of Irishmen who tired of traveling several miles afoot en masse to attend services in what would become nearby Georgetown or Staceyville. That year, the diocese sent Reverend Father McFadden to Melrose. Father McFadden had been raised himself in a Catholic orphanage near Belfast and had been sent half way around the world specifically to service his own people in Melrose.

A small committee of men formed to construct a church of their own. That spring construction began on a building that would be outgrown even before it was completed. While construction was under way, service was held by Father McFadden in a refurbished barn just outside of town. Each evening, railroad men led by brothers Finnian and Innis Keane worked by the light of their lanterns until the cathedral building was completed.

Men would come and help for a few hours after long 12 hour days on the railroad, but only Finnian and Innis were there every evening, joined by Innis Keane's oldest born son, 10 year old Collin. The brothers were devout religious men who gave their last penny and drop of sweat to the church. It was they two, and they alone with Collin, who would forego sleep for days upon end to see the structure completed before snow fell in the bottom.

Father McFadden worked with the Keanes on many evenings, but missed just as often to work on other church business. At every mass however, he made mention of the Keanes and their devotion. The

Reverend Father was not only busy writing and studying for his next performance while the men worked, but was day and night constructing the foundations of another sort.

The real foundations of the Catholic church of that day were not made of wood or stone or brick or mortar. The true power of the church lay in the people. For, it was the church that fed the hungry and clothed the poor and housed the homeless. It was the church that provided the youth with an education and the people with protection and counsel instead of the state. In immigrant communities especially, the church served as government, legal advisor, community center, and employment referral service.

The success of an individual amongst the flock bolstered the church's income which could be used to provide for those less fortunate. The parishioners would come to rely upon the church for all of their needs from birth to death. In return, the church would direct them in how to vote, who to hire, where to shop…everything.

When the railroads and mines sought to cut wages or experienced a particularly gruesome accident at the faults of the owners themselves, it was the church where they would turn with sizeable donations to quell any uprisings. In return, the church might be so inclined as to deliver a powerful sermon on the rewards that come in the afterlife to those who serve the lord AND their employers obediently in this world.

Within a few years of the establishment of the church, Reverend Father McFadden had so cemented the centralized power of the Melrose Catholic Church that long after the main thrust of the railroad and their Pinkertons had moved on, Irish Catholics continued to be the sole proprietors of every business in town. Between the church itself and the continued brute physical nature of the recently immigrated Irish, their growing community became an enclave hostile to outsiders who did not share similar backgrounds and beliefs.

The Irish Immigrants who had settled Melrose had grown accustomed, since their arrival in the country, to being mistreated and abused in every conceivable way. They had been taken advantage of and chased from one community to the next. Finally, here, in Melrose, they had found among the slow rolling Iowa hills what nowhere else had offered them. Melrose was a place to call their very own and once the influence of outsiders had been driven out by the Pinkerton men, they aimed to keep it their own.

For his own part, Father McFadden sought to help them keep it that way as well. So long as the Irish Catholics held sway over the area, he could hold sway over the Irish Catholics. His church would continue to be the center of the community and the premier local political power in nearly every conceivable way. Even as the railroad moved on, Melrose continued to be a rail service hub and employ hundreds of workers. And even as the railroad construction itself disappeared over the westward horizon to points unknown, most of the Irish stayed on in what had become their home.

As railroad construction went, the coal mines moved in to Southern Iowa and hundreds more Irish came with it. They too discovered a place unlike any other they had encountered. By 1890, Melrose had truly become Little Ireland. Of the thirty plus businesses that prospered in the town, including three hotels, all of them were owned and operated by Irishmen; every single one. Among the almost 1,000 residents, only half a dozen were not Irish Catholic.

The church, and the community, thrived and prospered with the booming of the mining operations. Throughout the mining states, the coal mine operators were a force to be reckoned with. They would come to control every aspect of the lives of their employees and the communities in which they lived. Everywhere, except for Melrose that is. There, in the little rural valley in Southern Iowa, the Reverend Father McFadden sat atop the throne of a community so well organized that not even the mine operators would think of going against his will.

Those who did not bow to the desires of the church in Melrose soon found themselves out of business, out of town, or much, much worse. In a time and place amongst men who resolved all issues with their fists, the Reverend Father need only utter words of support or admonishment to his parishioners about anyone, and swift reward or punishment fell upon them.

In 1897 when the neighboring operators sought to end the threat of the formation of a union amongst their employees, they did so by delivering hundreds of African American former slaves and prisoners from Alabama. It was Father McFadden himself who delivered the ultimatum to the coal company executives.

"Monroe is an Irish County, gentlemen," He was heard to say, "Remove these foul men from our county immediately or prepare for a war with every Irishman in Southern Iowa."

What he had not been heard to say that day, but what had been the true thrust of his conversation had been that the company need not worry about unions or strikes or any more loss of property. They need only remove the non-Irish laborers from the county and pay tribute to the church like every other area business did. Deliver unto the church a tribute and all of your worries shall melt away. Do it not, and you will be able to see the plumes of smoke from your burning operations all the way from Chicago.

It was a shakedown, Melrose style. In the end, the coal operators paid the church and sent the blacks to another town in Illinois to break a strike in friendlier territory. Father McFadden delivered his sermon about the great victory of the Irish and God for having run the black heathens out of their midst. He was hailed as a hero. He went on to preach that day about the church being the only true authorized representative of good Irish Catholics. "Any outsiders coming round HERE talking about THEIR unions, had ought well to be run out of the county just like the church has done with the black devils! For as we have seen here, invite one devil into our midst, and others are certain to follow!"

To the families of Melrose, all of whom had personally been helped at one time or another by Father McFadden, the community was their heaven upon earth. Father McFadden was their personal emissary to God. He was no longer followed or loved by his parishioners, he was worshipped.

One local youth even purchased his first team of horses and a wagon using the adoration of Father McFadden. He was able to do so from funds earned by drawing and selling charcoal pictures of none other than the Reverend Father McFadden. Soon, every home in the area had pictures of Father McFadden displayed prominently upon their walls, often beside the Virgin Mary herself!

When Father McFadden heard of this and saw one of the drawings, he called upon the boy and admonished him. His speech to the young man was not about the sins of pride or vanity, but the duty of every good Catholic to tax his own earnings on behalf of the church. Only after the boy had relinquished the required funds to the good Father, had he told the lad what a fine artist he was.

Chapter 5   The Sins of the Father

The Keane family had done well for themselves as church founding fathers in their own right. While both Finnian and Innis had passed during the 1890's, their large families had continued to benefit from the personal relationships with Father McFadden and their devoted role to the founding and construction of the church.

Young Collin Keane, who had worked with his father and his uncle each day to construct the original church building, would grow to become a master carpenter. Collin Keane continued to donate count-less hours to the church that he loved. His devotion to God, Father McFadden, and the church was second to no one in the community. As a result, whenever parishioners required carpentry, they turned first, as good Catholics should, to Collin. For if his hands were fine enough to serve the Lord then surely they were suitable to work on their homes and businesses as well.

By 1900, Melrose had become a boom town. The Melrose Catholic Church had grown to accommodate a congregation of almost a thousand regular attendees. During the summer months, they would travel by foot to a shady meadow filled with Oak trees amongst an open pasture. There, they would meet with the members of the Georgetown and Staceyville Catholic Churches which serviced the large Irish Catholic community in and around the county seat of Albia, Iowa.

The Reverend Fathers of all three churches would usually attend and give open air mass to huge crowds followed by a group picnic. It was an opportunity for the congregations to view the overall numbers within their own ranks in the county and feel first hand, the power of the church as a result of these numbers. It was during these picnic outings that major business deals were struck effecting commerce throughout the county and beyond.

It was during one such mass in June of the year 1900, that Collin Keane chose to stay behind and repair the deteriorating window sills on the original church building that he had helped his father build thirty years before. Since then, the original structure had been converted into a portion of the new school and orphanage. It had been intended to serve as only a school, but as the church began to come upon more roving children, the school auditorium was converted to more permanently house the wayward souls. The nuns who also lived on the premises and taught school by day would be called upon by the Lord, and Father McFadden, to pull double duty and care for the growing number of orphans at night as well.

For his own part, Father McFadden also served as headmaster of the school and orphanage. It was a seemingly noble gesture made by a devout soul for him to do so. For no one would expect the Reverend Father of such a large congregation to take on so much. It was yet another saintly act by Father McFadden. It only reinforced that he was worthy of the adoration lavished upon him by his devoted followers.

Collin Keane had gathered his tools and walked with his box along the empty town street. As he walked along, he admired the colorful sky and the beautiful songs of birds that could be heard all around him. Usually you could hardly hear the song birds over the hustle and bustle of the busy Melrose background noise. The voices of neighbors talking, the sound of horse hooves and wagon wheels, and the sounds of children running and playing left the entire Melrose bottom awash in noise. But on this night, Collin could only hear the songbirds, as the entire town had packed up their picnic baskets and rode or walked along the road to the beautiful meadow where the evening outdoor mass was being held.

He regretted missing the mass as he enjoyed the opportunity to relax and visit with his fellow man, rejoicing in the words of God delivered under the trembling shade trees. It was a nice idea the Reverend Father had come up with to hold the outdoor mass and they had become major events in the lives of Monroe County Irish Catholics.

To a master carpenter like Collin, it required a chapel built by the loving hands of craftsmen to experience the full glory of God. To him, even the most beautiful building in the world that was built by man was imperfect and men required it to remind themselves of their own imperfections. They could only try to work toward perfection and please the Lord with their efforts. In following this belief, Collin strove, as his father had before him, to please the Lord through his work on the buildings constructed to serve Him. It was why he took such pride in working late into the evening, and why he never accepted a penny in payment for his service.

The Lord would know that when the rest of his fellow men were picnicking and enjoying the evening, that Collin was still working to serve Him the best way that he knew how. Beyond his private sacrifice though, Collin also knew that the nuns and the children would all be gone on this evening. He would be able to work late into the evening and not worry that the pounding of his nails might keep people awake. What he hadn't known was that Father McFadden himself had stayed behind that night as well, called upon by the Lord he had said, to stay and care for a sick child. The nuns had praised him for his selflessness and went on their way to the mass, promising to praise his name for staying behind.

As Collin retrieved a ladder from a small tool shed he had built a few years earlier, he noticed that the time was upon him again to paint the eaves of the old chapel. As he placed his ladder against the building alongside the window he grasped his hammer and a small flat bar. The old hammer had worn smooth to fit his grip. He admired how it felt in his hand, like an old pair of well worn boots that hugged and caressed the foot. There had been times when he had carried his hammer into the kitchen for dinner and didn't even realize he was still carrying it.

Climbing the ladder, he reached out to the middle of the window and set his bar in place to begin stripping the wood. But even before he struck the bar set with his hammer behind the wood, his eye caught the movement from inside. The widowed Mrs. Navin had stitched every thread of the beautiful window coverings, but she had measured them wrong for the older windows in the chapel and the top foot of the window remained open to the world. Mostly, it worked well to allow in the extra light. But on this evening, it enabled Collin to see into the window and view the shadows in the flickering of the lantern light inside.

His hammer fell from his hand as he peered inside. As it dropped, it caught the bottom of the window sill and the bang caused the figures inside to turn and look directly at him. He saw the faces of a boy of about thirteen and Father McFadden himself staring back at him. Both of them were nude and had been engaged in unspeakable acts. As Collin looked on, stunned, he noticed not that his ladder was beginning to lean with him. Before the figures inside could move, he fell to the ground with the ladder in tow.

"Brother Keane!" He heard the voice of Father McFadden call to him, but he scrambled to his feet as he crawled away from the building and out from under the ladder.

"Brother Keane!" He heard the voice scream again as he ran full speed across the chapel lawn and down the dirt road. Collin did not look back. He could not. He only ran, as fast as his legs could carry him. He was 37 years old that day and he had not run with such vigor since he was a boy. He ran past his own home and on through the empty roads to the edge of town. He ran on, and kept on running until he passed through a small stretch of woods and into the opening of the cemetery.

At the cemetery, he finally slowed and came upon the familiar marker of his father's grave. He walked to it, fell to his knees before it, and wept like a child. He was angry and hurt and upset and sobbed to his father's ghost for answers. But even more than that, for reasons that he could not begin to understand, he was afraid. Afraid of what, he knew not, but fear coursed through his veins and left every muscle in his body tingling as if from sharp needle pricks.

Chapter 6   Retribution

It was very late that night when Collin finally crawled into bed beside his wife. He watched her by the light of the moon while she slept. In the other room, the four young sons she had bore him also slept quiet as mice. They always slept soundly thus following an outdoor mass. The children all ran about playing games until well after dark, and many collapsed into their parent's arms on the walk back home.

It was out of love for these sleeping lambs and the woman beside him in the bed that Collin had concluded upon his course of action. He knew the power of the church and of the Reverend Father McFadden. He knew that his own word against that of a well loved clergyman would hold little weight regardless. So, he had concluded, why put my family through it all? No. He would not have it. He would not be called a liar and have his name dragged through the mud all across the county. Besides, it was not becoming of a good Catholic to even speak of such things openly.

But a good Catholic he was, and he owed it to God, and his own conscience, to at least seek out the Reverend Father of Staceyville or Georgetown and ask for their counsel in the matter. It was the duty of all good Catholics to see that no great decision or moral dilemma be taken headlong without the counsel of the church and the influence of the Lord. The Lord sent many such tests before His subjects to make certain they were fit to handle it appropriately and not make rash judgments. For only the Lord Himself was fit to do so, and whenever men attempted it, things always ended in calamitous disaster. So, he had decided, he would avoid the Reverend Father for now, not mention what he had seen to anyone, and seek out the counsel in the morrow.

Morning would not arrive soon enough for Collin. He tossed and turned the night away as his mind replayed what his eyes had witnessed. Had his eyes deceived him? No. He was certain of what he had seen. Was it possible, even remotely so, that he had misunderstood what he had witnessed? No. There could be no misunderstanding it. His mind could not have dreamed up such a thing or considered that such a possibility could have even existed. Such were the thoughts in his mind as it raced through the night, turning the thing over and over in his weary head.

Outside as the church bells tolled 5:00am, Collin was only beginning to feel his eyes grow heavy enough to consider sleep. As his eyelids finally relinquished and closed, the beating came upon the door. BAM, BAM, BAM, BAM came the four quick, hard poundings.

"Keane!" the voice demanded, "Open up in there!" The deep voice and thick Irish brogue was followed by another succession of four fist poundings. "Keane! It's Sheriff Nolan. You'll be best to open your door!"

Collin, still pulling his suspenders over his shoulders, opened the door if only to stop the yelling and the pounding from waking his whole family and the entire neighborhood to boot.
"Yes, what is it Sheriff?" Even as he spoke, Collin looked at the eyes of the small group of men with the town Sheriff, Quinn Nolan.

Beside Sheriff Nolan stood Kieran O'Donnell, the owner of the Melrose Savings & Loan. Behind these two stood four others, all of them friends and church elders. None of them in the rear of the group would look him in the eye however. They merely stood there uncomfortably fidgeting about and gawking at their own feet.

"We've come to give you this," Sheriff Nolan handed him a document of fine parchment with flowing handwritten calligraphy on it. He had only seen writing like that before on his own marriage certificate from his wedding some years before. He glanced up at the men once more confused and still wiping the sleep from his eyes then looked back and read the document.

<u>Writ of Vitandus Excommunicato</u>

Be it known that on this, the 18th day of September in the year of Our Lord Nineteen Hundred A.D., that the Holy Roman Catholic Church of East Melrose, Iowa hath issued for one Collin Ennis Keane this Writ of Vitandus Excommunicato for his crimes against the church and against Our Lord God. Upon the receipt of numerous complaints and allegations, and in light of evidence which hath emerged following the same, the Church hath deemed it most appropriate to issue said Writ En Latae Sententiae, of immediate sentencing. The Sins, Crimes, and Heresy known to have been committed have left no recourse to the church but to protect the souls of our congregation by issuing this Writ of Vitandus Excommunicato. Aside from expulsion from receiving Communion by the Church, for the sanctity of the very souls of the innocents the Writ of Vitandus has been issued as he is to be avoided by all other Catholics in person and in businesses. None shall be granted Communion who shall seek to provide company, food, or shelter. For those who aid in Evil are the same in the eyes of the Lord, and the Church as the Evildoer himself.

Reverend Father McFadden

Collin looked at the men in confusion. It could not be so. "Why?" He asked. "What have I done?"

"These are your eviction papers," Kiernan O'Donnell handed him two pieces of paper and stepped back nervously. "The bank can no longer honor your note."

"You need to get your family and get out of the house Collin," Sheriff Nolan stated, "These men will remove your things."

"What?" Collin's confusion turned to anger, "No, you don't understand..."

"Daddy, what's wrong?" Came the voice of his nine year old son, Merril from the doorway of the kitchen. Behind him stood his brothers and mother, all wiping away the sleep from their eyes and looking bewildered.

"It's nothing, son," Collin replied, "Just..."

Just then a heavy blow struck Collin across the side of his head. As he turned back toward the men, he could see that Sheriff Nolan's face had turned mean in the instant he had looked away. Collin raised his hand to defend himself, but it was too late to stop the second blow of the sappy from landing squarely across his forehead.

The thick leather strip of the sappy made it flexible, but the lead beads that filled the leather head of it made it formidable. It had become the weapon of choice by law enforcement officers throughout fighting immigrant mining communities as the victim could easily be rendered unconscious without the bloodshed produced by nightsticks. And unlike guns, individuals on the receiving end of a sappy would be able to work the next day for the mines and pay the sheriff a hefty fine for having troubled him.

"No. You don't understand!" Sheriff Nolan yelled as he swung his sappy once more, watching as Collin's knees buckled from beneath him. As the third blow struck his head on the way to the ground, Collin slipped from consciousness. The men drug him out into the mud road amidst the sounds of his crying children and screaming wife who rushed to his side and knelt in the mud around his limp body.

As they wept and Collin began to stir, their belongings were being thrown into the yard and the street around them. Meara watched helplessly as her grandmother's furniture and dishes broke one on top the other as the men threw them out of the doors and windows. The banker had pleaded with them to be careful not to break any more glass, but the men were delighted in their work and continued to throw family heirlooms through the closed windows. She could only grasp on to her infant son and watch in horror at the destruction of her home and her belongings.

Neighbors had emerged from their homes and questioned Sheriff Nolan about what was becoming of the Keanes. What he and Kiernan O'Donnell had told them was anyone's guess, but the word that Meara could hear being repeated was "excommunicated."

By the time Collin had come to enough to sit up, the Sheriff and Kieran O'Donnell and the others had all gone. He awoke to discover every worldly possession of theirs piled in the front yard in broken heaps and his family all sobbing. Just then his cousin drove by in a wagon and looked upon the weeping family.

"Ryan!" Collin Shouted to him. "Ryan, please come help us!"

"Vitandus Excommunicato!" Ryan proclaimed, glaring in disgust at his flesh and blood, and spat onto the ground as he drove on past them.

It would be the same with all of them. Lifelong friends and relatives alike would shun his entire family. No Writ of Vitandus Excommunicato had been issued in this country in anyone's memory, so they knew that it must be the result of atrocities against humanity and God himself. Rumors and speculations flew about what his actual crimes had been, but no one stopped for an instant to question Father McFadden about their validity or their details. They only praised him all the more for diligently protecting the people of the county and for protecting their own innocence by keeping the details un-spoken.

Thirty years and two generations of devout religious fervor and unparalleled devotion had ended in an instant. Collin Keane, his wife and four sons were cast out of the church and their home and left without a friend in the entire world who would dare to help them against the will of God. No one would so much as speak to him now, let alone entertain his story about Father McFadden and the real reason behind the excommunication. Collin knew that to even speak of such a thing to anyone now, would most certainly result in his own untimely death at the hands of his own people.

The good Reverend Father McFadden's plan had worked perfectly.

Chapter 7   One Man's Trash

Collin Keane and family had fled the town of Melrose, taking with them only what could be carried. For the most part, their belongings had been ruined by the men who'd come to evict them, so there was precious little to carry anyhow. Believing that the safety of his children had been in jeopardy, he did not allow them to rest until they were well outside of the town.

They had been caught in the woods in a rainstorm the first night. As a result, his youngest son, Tomas, had taken ill the next morning. Desperate for shelter first and foremost, Collin led his family to the nearest place he knew of not already settled by Irish Catholics who may seek to do him harm, the county trash dump. There he was able to scavenge the materials to build a small shelter on that day.

The trash dump was a temporary stopping point for the family. But as Tomas was too ill to travel, Collin kept his mind occupied by improving their shelter. Within a week, Tomas had fallen asleep one evening shivering and failed to wake up the next morning. He was dead. They stayed on to bury the boy on a nearby hilltop and grieved. While they grieved, Collin kept on working to improve their shelter and before long the assemblages of a house began to form around them.

Collin had insisted on leaving the area entirely, but with the loss of their son, the family became essentially immobile. For weeks the family barely cared enough to find food to feed itself with. Collin remained productive, but only to keep his mind occupied. Scavenging for just the right piece here and the perfect metal to shear off for makeshift nails there was the only thing that kept him sane. Not sanity like we know of it, but the kind of sanity that barely qualifies itself as such. It was survival sanity, ensuring that he kept breathing for one more day. The project planned for tomorrow would ensure that he would be around when the day arrived and had *something* that kept him putting one foot in front of the other until his own will to live returned.

What is unbearable or unthinkable on one day has a way of becoming routine the next. It is that very quality that has allowed for the human condition to carry on through famines, plagues, floods, and changing climates. As humans live each day, no matter how they live, they come to depend upon their individual routines.

As the autumn leaves fell and the cold winds began to blow signaling the coming of winter, the family cut wood. They would go in the spring, they told themselves. But as the spring came and passed they found that they had settled into their new condition somewhat. Even if they hadn't come to rely upon their new routines, neither of the parents had the will it required to set out for parts unknown and begin anew. Where would they go anyhow? What would become of them when they got there?

Here, at least, the family could keep scavenging the dump. It provided them with the roof over their heads, and scrap materials to trade in Albia and Chariton with the Methodist business owners who cared not about the Catholic excommunication. At times, regrettably too often, the dump also provided them with their only source of food. If not directly through the occasional discarded animal or tavern scrapings, then always there were the rats. What began as an act of winter desperation and a food source that came to them each night in droves in their own home quickly became a staple of life.

Thus became the way of their life; living amongst the rats, picking through the mountains of fresh garbage each day, and living in constant fear of their own kind. Collin made them all hide whenever he recognized Irish Catholics approaching. To him, they were a constant threat. To the Irish Catholics, the Keanes became the 'Devils of the Dump.' Amongst the townspeople, the Keanes were a staple of scary children's bedtime stories warning them to stay clear and behave, lest they be fell upon and eaten or the like by the Devils of the Dump. Their own relatives who remained in the area had disowned them and referred to them as "The *other* Keanes," inferring that they were of no relation and probably of Protestant descent in the Old Country.

Life was hard on Meara and Collin who could remember the good times. But it was hardest of all on their eldest son, Merril. For Merril remembered the good times as well. He remembered his friends in the town and the church outings and he remembered going to school. His father had told him that it was out of the question for him to ever return to the school and Merril had come to resent him for that, among other things. He never really knew what his father had done, or what had really happened. He only knew that before they had lived, but now they only survived, and his father was somehow to blame for it all.

Chapter 8   Devils of the Dump

1910 had witnessed an explosion in the population of Melrose and all of Monroe County as the result of major expansions in coal mining operations. The county which today boasts of only some 8,000 souls was then home to over 25,000. More people meant more of everything, including garbage, and collecting valuable metals and other salvageable goods from the dump became more and more lucrative with each passing day.

After years of barely surviving, the salvaging of other's garbage began to show results that actually produced a bit of revenue beyond the hand to mouth existence that Merril had known his entire life. It was this boon in the "industry" that was the only thing that kept 19 year old Merril at home and living and working each day at the life he had grown to despise, with the father he had come to resent.

Between 1900 and 1910, Merril watched the health of his two remaining younger brothers deteriorate. Whether it was from living at the dump and breathing the thick black smoke of the fires there or eating rats and garbage he did not know, but he knew that it must be the result of living there. Both of them had been laid to rest beside Tomas in what had become a rapidly growing family plot.

In 1911 Merril's mother caught a virus that had been going around and she died several days later with a horrible fever and half mad. The night before she had died, she had laid awake, screaming incoherent sentences about the Catholic Church, a priest by the name of Father McFadden, who himself had recently died, and her own husband, Collin. They had buried her in the same family plot on the hillside and his father never spoke of her again.

In fact, Collin would rarely speak to anyone at all after that. He began spending more and more time in a small shed he had built to store scrap in, until he just didn't return to the slightly larger shanty that served as their house. Whatever instincts that had driven him to keep his sanity had finally given way. He would spend the rest of his days rarely speaking directly to anyone, even his own son.

Collin would only wander about sorting through garbage. He could be heard, however, cursing and talking to himself. One resident of Melrose, upon returning from a trip to the dump reported to have seen Collin catch a live rat by the tail and eat it whole. It would be this story and a hundred stories like it that kept alive the fear and loathing for the 'Devils of the Dump' in residents too new or too young to have ever even heard about the excommunication or remembered a time when the family was a respected part of the church and community.

For as much as Collin had lived in fear for himself and his family, Merril Keane lived in a state of anger. He hated his own father for having ruined any chance he'd had at a normal life and a happy childhood. He hated him for the death of his brothers. He even hated him for having lost his mind. It suited him well that Collin no longer attempted to speak to him directly. It also suited him well that none of the townspeople did so either.

As much as he hated the dump and all that it had come to represent, the *business* itself was sustaining him better every day, and it was the only life that he really knew. The population explosion had done so well for him in fact, that he was able to purchase ten acres from a nearby Methodist farmer friend.

He quickly set to work building a proper house like the ones in the towns. Merril could now leave his father to haunt the shanties and sheds alone and by so doing, set himself a step above from whence he had come and a bit further apart from the Devils of the Dump. He may continue to live off of garbage, but that did not mean he was doomed to live *in* it.

Following the completion of his new home, Merril began spending more of his evenings in Albia at the taverns and saloons. It was there, through the clouded eyes of a whiskey drunk, that he met his wife to be, Sarah. They had little to offer one another in the way of looks or conversation, but they both had one thing in common. They both had been shunned by those around them. Sarah, for her part, had conceived a child out of wedlock, and refusing to be sent away to deliver the thing as an orphan and future ward of the church, she had kept her baby.

Merril had never learned how to love from his parents or anyone else. The best chance that he had at ever learning about it at all had passed from this world with his brothers. But he liked that she too had been shunned. He liked that by being with her, he could stick another thorn in the side of 'polite society.' It was a relationship born out of spite more than anything. Late in the fall of 1916, between them and their unholy union, there would be born another son to call their own...Aidan Frances Keane.

Chapter 9 Hats

Locals who knew the tale of the family said that Aidan had been damned from the start. His father's entire family and his own mother both had been excommunicated from the Holy Roman Church. To add insult to injury, they say that the couple had never married in any church at all. Not even the law of the State of Iowa had cause to recognize the two. It was even rumored that the child had been born on Halloween night of all nights. In the eyes of the Lord and all who lived by His word, Aidan was the most unholy sort of bastard child that could be imagined.

To the world, Aidan was the bastard child of the Devils of the Dump. To his father, though, he was the hope of the future. Through Aidan, Merril figured, all wrongs of the past could be righted. If he stayed strict enough with the child, and drove him hard enough, then he, at least, would not be condemned to the sort of life that Merril had been forced to endure.

So while Aidan's older half brother, Doran, was brought along with Merril to sort through the garbage at a very young age, Aidan stayed at home with his mother. His father swore that Aidan would not live in fear of the men who were no better than him. He would not spend his life sorting through *their* garbage either.

"No Catholic sons of whores are any better than you boy," Aidan remembered his father saying. "Don't you ever even think it so. And don't you ever let any of them think it either, no matter what. You hear me?"

"Yes sir," he would reply obediently.

While Doran and Merril packed their lunches and headed off for the nearby dump, Aidan stayed behind with his mother, who at her husband's insistence, began to teach her son arithmetic and Latin at the age of four. By the age of five he could read well above his age, and by his sixth birthday, he could recite a growing number of Latin phrases.

And so it came to pass on his sixth year of life that Aidan was led into Melrose by his father. He had walked with his father a hundred times as of the evening to the town and knew the trail through the woods and across the bottom well. While the day had been for learning Latin, the evening walks with his father were for learning of the Catholics. He learned through his father that the Catholics were never to be feared, but loathed.

"Never trust those Bible thumpin' sons of whores," he'd say to his young son. "They're lower than snakes in the grass and look down their noses at everyone in this world that aint just like them. But don't you ever let em' look down their noses at you, boy. You're a Keane, and there aint nobody better than a Keane. You understand me?"

"Yes sir," the boy would always reply.
Aidan's father grabbed his hand and clenched it tightly as they walked through the doors of the school. It was the Catholic school for boys, the only school in the town, and the one that Merril himself had attended as a small boy before the incident. His father had lived in fear and never allowed him to have normal life. But Aidan was going to be different. Aidan was going to prove to the world that the Keanes were as good as the rest. He would show them come hell or high water that the Keanes were a proud people who feared no one.

Aidan looked in amazement at the size of the building. It seemed to go on forever in each direction. He hesitated as they opened the entrance doors to the school and marveled at the size of them. The tall, dark, heavy wooden double doors were encased in a thick stone doorway. He was thinking that it must have took a hundred men to put the stone up there so high and another hundred to lift the doors into place when his father jerked him on through and into the building.

Inside, his eyes adjusted to the light, or lack thereof and he saw a small group of boys staring at him as they disappeared into a hallway door. It was his first good look at genuine, for sure, Irish Catholic boys. While they didn't appear to be the monsters that his father had made them out to be, fear shot down his spine nonetheless and he could feel his small stomach begin to churn.

He was still reeling from having laid eyes upon the other children when his father smacked the back of his head. "Take your hat off in a building boy," he'd said as Aidan picked his hat up off the finely polished floor, "aint polite to wear it inside."

Walking into the door marked "office" Aidan got his first glimpse of nuns. They appeared to be women, same as the rest of them he'd seen, but all dressed up in long black dresses and the funniest hats he'd ever heard tell of. He wondered why they had their hats on inside the building anyways, and he couldn't wait to get home and tell Doran about those funny hats. He'd have to try his damnedest to remember them so he could draw a picture to show to Doran. They'd get a great laugh about it later.

"I want to enroll my boy in this here school," Merril told the nun behind the desk inside the office door.

"Very well then," replied the nun.

"Name?" She asked after producing a sheet of paper from her desk.

"I'm Merril Keane," he replied, squeezing his clenched hat tightly in his hand. The older nun in the back of the office glanced up at him and grimaced, then whispered something to another nun beside her.

"The name of the boy. What is the boy's name?" The nun at the desk irritably replied.

"Oh, *him*. We call him Aidan," Merril replied proudly, almost expecting a confrontation of some sort with the nuns right then and there. "Aidan Keane is his name."

But there was no confrontation right then and there. In fact, even the old nun who appeared to recognize the name and had whispered something to another nun said nothing to cause a stir that morning. Merril walked Aidan home with a proud jaunt that afternoon. He had looked the demons in the eye and won. His boy would go to school among them and prove that the Keanes were afraid of nothing, and there was none better or smarter among the Catholics or anyone else for that matter.

"Did you see the hats them women was wearing Papa?" Aidan asked as they walked home.

"Yes, I did," Replied the elder Keane.

"Them sure was funny hats, wasn't they Papa?" Aidan said, looking at his Father for a sign that he too thought they were funny hats.

"You be weary of them hats, boy. The folks who wear em will be no friend," he replied with a grimace.

Chapter 10   Shirts

The following morning Aidan's father called him to breakfast. He leaped out of bed and hurriedly dressed himself, not wanting to be late for his first day of school. Finally, his day had come to prove himself to his father and make him proud. After quickly eating, he grabbed the lunch that his mother had made him and headed for the door.

"You remember what I told you, boy!" His father called after him.

"Yes sir. I will papa!" Replied young Aidan as the door closed behind him.

As Aidan walked through the woods toward town, he tried to remember all of the things that his father had taught him. He felt a knot inside of his stomach that tightened when he thought of the boys he had seen the day before. This day was different to him it seemed. Even the nuns with their funny hats seemed frightening to him. The huge doors that just the day before had seemed so incredible and awe inspiring left him with a feeling of ominous foreboding as he approached them alone.

He had been so excited the night before that he had barely slept. He must have woken up a hundred times, he reckoned, and sat up looking at the window for signs of first light. What had begun as nervous excitement however quickly turned to tension and fear as he approached the school building. He saw groups of boys walking in through the big wooden doors which had been propped open (presumably by some very strong adult). His nerves got the best of him when he noticed that all of the boys wore crimson colored shirts and green ties. His shirt was grey and his tie (which had been his father's before him) was supposed to be black, but most of the color had faded years ago. Now it was a putrid grey that almost matched his shirt, but mostly, they just looked dirty in comparison to the bright crimson worn by the other boys. He thought he might be sick to his stomach the way it was churning all about, but he pushed himself to enter the building anyhow.

Inside he went to the same office where he had been the day before with his father. There he was issued two yellow shirts by the older nun who had been in the back of the room whispering the day before.

"You'll need to put one of these on before you go to class," she told him.

"But all the other boys have red ones," he said.

"Don't you back talk to me, heathen," she barked. "You'll do as you're told while in this school. You should have stayed put in the junk yard with the rats where you belong. Now put it on and get to classroom number four!" She glared at him and with a trembling finger she pointed across the hallway to the changing room.

If he had been nervous before, he was terrified after the exchange. He wanted to turn and run out the door. Run home and never look back, but his father would not have him. He imagined that he'd be beaten within an inch of his life if he left now. He knew how important this was to his father that he did well, so he went into the coat room to change.

Inside the room there was a flurry of activity. Two older boys stood near the window sharing a cigarette and blowing the smoke out the window. A few other boys were looking at some comics one of them held and were laughing. At the mirror a kid worked on combing back his slick, greasy hair while another one in the group reading the comics kept reaching out to mess it up again.

40

"Knock it off Wilbur! You son of a bitch! I'm gonna kill you if you don't..." Just then the boy stopped mid-sentence as he noticed Aidan standing in the doorway looking scared and confused. "Well, looky what we have here fellas," The boy said, eyeing the young boy in the doorway who stood grasping tightly to his yellow shirts as his face turned pale as a ghost.

"A God damned yellow shirt!" Another boy said as they walked toward him.

"What are you boy?" Another asked.

"What am I? I'm a Keane!" Aidan exclaimed, grasping for an answer to a question he didn't understand.

"Hey, Orrin," one of them called out behind him, "This here yellow shirt says he's a Keane just like you!"

From out of the back of the room, one of the older boys who had been sharing a cigarette stepped forward and looked Aidan up and down.

"He ain't no fucking Keane. God damned liar is what he is." The older boy said as he knocked the shirts to the floor out of Aidan's grip. Before he could turn to run away, the older boy had pushed him into the wall. Aidan's head struck the hard surface with a loud thud.

He couldn't tell if it was really as loud as it had sounded, or if he had just heard the sound of his head breaking apart from being slammed into the wall. As he struggled to stand straight up and get his balance, the older boy's fist landed square on his nose knocking him to the floor. The ceiling spun around above his head as he felt the boot smash into his stomach. He curled up tightly into a ball and tried desperately to cover his face as he cried and begged for the boy to stop or someone to help him.

He could not have said for sure how many times he had been struck while he lay there. He only knew that at some point the beating had ceased. When he dared to look up through his teary eyes he could see spinning above him, along with the rest of the room, was the old nun. Next, he felt a pain in his ear and he thought the whole side of his head would be ripped off as the nun pulled him to his feet.

"You two will come with me to the office!" She yelled as she pulled the two boys across the hallway by their ears.

Inside the office, she had them both sit in a chair facing her as she made her way to her own chair behind a desk.

"Orrin," she looked sternly at the boy who had just beaten him, "tell me what has just happened."

"I don't know Reverend Mother," the boy replied sheepishly, "he just sort of jumped at me. I tried to stop him and he just kept swinging and cursing at..."

"That's a lie!" Aidan shouted.

"Enough!" The old nun screamed, and she reached across with a thick cut of willow and slapped Aidan's arm with it.

Aidan, still holding his head and crying, pulled his stinging forearm close and looked at her with horror. He was hurt and scared and confused before, and now she too was hurting him. He had thought that he would be safe once they had made it out of the bathroom. That it all was over and the hurting would stop. He was wrong.

"Orrin, return to your class young man and tell Sister Margaret that you are to have no outdoor break today."

"Yes, Reverend Mother," the boy said sweetly and timidly as he high tailed it out of the room and quickly disappeared down the hallway.

"As for you, you heathenish bastard," her beady dark eyes glared at him through her thick glasses from out behind her gnarled, leathery aged face. It was the sort of face that required years of anger and frowning to create. It was a face that Aidan would come to know all too well though and in short order, learn to hate with every bone in

42

his frail tiny body. "You will rise and come with me. And not a peep out of you or so help me, I will beat the devil from you on this day."

Her thick Irish brogue and small frame could have caused one to mistake her for someone's granny, Aidan had thought. But there was a horrible cruelness in her eyes that he had not before seen in anyone. He followed her down the hallway to a large room full of tables and chairs.

"You sit right there heathen," she said, pointing her bony wrinkled finger at a seat by itself in the front of the big room. "You stay right there and don't you move from that spot until you're told to or so help me. And you will put your shirt on as you have been told!" She said and then disappeared back into the hallway at a brisk pace, carrying the whipping stick vertically behind her back as if meant to sneak up on her next victim.

Aidan sat and bawled, holding his arm, rubbing his bruised ribs, and feeling the welt that had formed on the back of his head. "Why?" He said to himself over and over, but there was never an answer, just the sound of his wails, and the sniffles of his bloodied nose.

Sometime in the next hour or so, he remembered to put on his yellow shirt as he had been told. He used the grey one to finish cleaning the dried blood from out of his nostrils, but he couldn't tell how much was left on his face without a mirror or water to wash it with properly. He waited for what seemed like an eternity, but still no one came. He thought of getting up time and again, but for the now, no one was hurting him at least. He had best stay put, he reckoned, and do what he had been told.

After what seemed to the boy of not quite seven, to be an eternity, (but was really three hours) of sitting alone in the room, other boys began slowly filtering in. As they did, two sets of large doors opened up behind him and the boys began walking into one and emerging out the other set with plates of food. He had never been in a lunchroom before, but as the smells filled the air and caused his empty stomach to grumble in rebellion, he quickly figured out the purpose of the place.

43

Most children of the town had their own lunches sent with them from home to avoid all the greater tuition charged by the school, but the makeshift pieced together buildings also served as an orphanage, so there had to be a commonplace where meals could be served. When the room had slowly filled up with boys of all shapes and sizes, they one by one looked at the boy in the yellow shirt sitting alone at the head table and they knew what would be coming for him soon. They had seen this show before.

The yellow shirts were to identify the non-Catholics and the nuns showed them no quarter. The last yellow shirt that had attended that school was thirteen year old Leonard Patrika, son of a Polish miner who went there the year before. No one knows exactly why he had done it, but only days before the beginning of the new school year, Yellow Leonard, as the other students had called him, had taken his father's rifle and shot himself right in the heart.

Throughout the large open room, the children sat with their meals in front of them. Those who had brought their own from home, opened their tins and prepared their food stuffs, but none dared to take a bite. Instead, they leaned into one another's ears, looked at the boy in the front of the room, and whispered. Some glared at him, some exchanged words and giggled, and others laughed openly at Aidan. But there was no mistaking that all eyes were focused relentlessly upon him.

Tears of another sort ran down his cheeks, they were wrought not from the pain he had endured, but from sheer embarrassment. For he had never before been amongst so many boys in all of his life, let alone had them stare at him so. Indeed, he had really only ever played with his own brother Doran. He alone had been Aidan's best and only friend as a child. As much as no one desired to have their children playing with the Devils of the Dump, their own father would not be in the company of anyone save the two Non-Catholic neighbors they shared, and neither of them had young children about.

Aidan heard a hush fall over the room and listened as a mighty rustling occurred about him. As he peered out from behind his own hands he saw that every child in the room had risen to their feet. He heard the ominous quick paced hard shoes approach and hid his face once more. His body began to tremble as the footsteps seemed to have singled him out and grew ever near. He shook and quivered and the sounds of muffled sobs began to emanate from within the protective cocoon of his hands and arms that kept hidden his face and head. And then the footsteps ceased.

"Today, we have a heathen among us," the words of the Reverend Mother echoed through the back of the hall. "It is the call of a good Catholic to remain ever vigilant of the tests placed before us. The Godless bastard child you see here before you today has come here to try to tempt the souls of the righteous. Will ye be tempted? Today, he has lashed out at Orrin Keane himself. Tomorrow, only the Lord knows what evils he may try to unleash upon ye. Do not be tempted children! Do not be afraid for if the spirit of the Lord be in you, then you should fear no evil, nor be tempted by it. But hear me now, be ever vigilant. Do not turn your back nor let down your guard, for just as the Lord works in many mysterious ways, so does Satan seek to fool you. Let down your guard. Befriend him. Allow him into your heart or into your home and sure as St. Peter, he'll drag you back with him kicking and screaming to the depths of hell!"

"Now rise heathen, and prepare to feel the wrath of the Lord upon ye. Feel the sting of righteousness upon your shameful soul!" And with that she pulled Aidan up from his chair and pushed him half bent over the table. She then produced a long wooden paddle shaved of hickory and worn smooth by a lifetime of use. She counted each stinging blow as she swung back as far as her small arms could and then let loose again.

Aidan had no idea how many such swats he would receive. He tried desperately to keep his cries to himself as he was more concerned about the hundred sets of eyes upon him than the pain that each blow delivered. Try as he might though, he let loose an uncontrollable crying wail as each blow landed upon his buttocks. He sought to concentrate to endure it, but each blow sent pain coursing through his entire body and shattered his concentration. When the count reached ten, it stopped, but he let loose one more scream in cadence with the time that the eleventh would have struck.

When the eleventh blow did not arrive as planned for, the boys throughout the hall giggled and murmured. The Reverend Mother led Aidan through the crowded hall and to the office once more where he was left to sit the remainder of the day. In the morrow, he was told, he would have the opportunity to try and see if he could behave long enough to make it to an actual class. There would be no lunch for him, she had said, as his empty stomach might serve as a reminder of the empty depths of the pits of hell that he'd surely one day return to. Aidan wept silently.

Chapter 11   No Place Like Home

When school let out that afternoon, Aidan only stared at his shoes as he began the long walk home. Crossing the threshold of the school and out the large doors encased in huge stonework that had embodied so much hopeful anticipation only the day before, he tried not to hear the taunts of the boys who lay in wait outside. He only stared at his ragged shoes and kept walking hoping that they would drift into the distance behind him and stay in the past with the rest of the bad dream he'd had that day.

As he continued to walk, most of the voices did fade into the distance, but a few grew ever nearer. Finally, as he rounded the corner of the last block of the town and looked up, he could see the woods that marked the trail home. He turned to look over his shoulder and saw the three boys running up behind him.

"No!" He cried. But it was already too late, for one had let loose a tomato he'd stolen from a garden. It hit Aidan upside his cheek and the laughter and taunts only grew out of the stinging pain. "Please!" He cried, but the boys were upon him.

They encircled him and pushed him, calling him "Devil" and all sorts of other names he'd never heard of before. Finally he mustered the courage to look the boys in the eyes. Two of them were smiling and screaming, but one actually appeared more afraid than anything. The boy tried to mask his own fear with an angry look and taunts, but the fear still shone through.

Aidan was beaten, terrified, and cornered. Just then, he did the unthinkable. He pushed the largest of the three boys and turned toward the scared one and screamed at the top of his lungs. The scared boy turned to run and knocked his remaining partner off his balance. Aidan turned and ran into the woods. He kept running and didn't slow to look behind him. As far as he knew, they remained upon his heels like a pack of angry dogs. He imagined that they were running just a step behind him, only waiting for the moment he slipped or slowed his pace to finish him off like a wounded rabbit.

He ran through the woods until his lungs were on fire and then ran even harder. He ran across his father's wood lot and through his mother's garden. He ran through the yard and up the steps and across the porch. He ran inside the house and slammed the door behind him, falling to the floor out of breath.

His mother, father, and brother were all at home to greet him from his first day, and they all hurried around him. Gathering him up from the floor, his father inquired, "What is the matter with you boy? What has happened?"

But Aidan was too out of breath to complete a sentence. He could only form words at first. "Boys. Chased me. Hit me. Chased. Oh papa," he began to cry once more. "Don't make me go," he cried.

"I get it. You come with me boy," he said sternly.

Aidan's father helped him back out the door and led him to the back steps of the house where he had him sit to rest. His mother came out and gave him a tin cup with cool water in it. He drank it right down. It was the first drink he had all day. He hadn't even realized how dry his mouth had been until the water touched his lips. He thought he must've cried a river of tears that day at the school. Small wonder he drank down the big tin so fast.

"You wait here, boy," his father said and headed out toward the barn.

His mother rubbed Aidan's hair back. "It'll be alright," she said softly. "Your father knows what's best," she reassured him.

Aidan's father walked back across the lawn and as he neared he began to speak. "I am sorry boy. I truly am. But no son of Merril Keane is going to turn heel and run from any God damned weak minded Catholic son of a bitch!" And with that he produced a buggy whip and struck Aidan across the legs with it.

His mother lurched out instinctively and tried to stop her husband from swinging the whip a second time, but Merril shoved her to the ground. "Out of my way woman, or there will be two of you with something to cry about," he yelled at her.

Aidan could only curl tightly into his defensive ball and await the pain that was certain to follow. He deserved it sure as sin, he reckoned, for having let down his father. He had only wanted to make him proud that day, but he had failed him in every possible way. His father did not count his blows as the Reverend Mother had that day so Aidan didn't know how many times he hit him. He only knew that it lasted longer and hurt worse than anything else he had already endured.

When his father had finally emptied himself of his rage and tired, he only spoke thus; "If you meet your better amongst those Catholic sons of whores then so be it. But by God, you will stand and be bested then. I'll not have you hiding amongst other men's waste the rest of your life! You're a Keane! You'll learn to take the pain that comes to you or receive thrice of it from me." And with that he walked away and left his son curled in a ball alone with a sobbing mother who was too afraid to comfort him.

Chapter 12   Doran

Doran was three years older than Aidan, who would turn seven in a few months. Ten year old Doran had always been Aidan's protector and friend. Before being put to work at the dump with their father every day a few years back, the two had been inseparable.

Merril had always tried to claim both of the boys as his own, but his handful of Methodist friends could tell otherwise. This, they had kept to themselves of course, but Aidan's green eyes and sandy blonde hair were in stark contrast to Doran's light complexion and fiery thick head of red hair. In the heat of the summer months Aidan would brown up until he could have passed as an Indian, whereas poor Doran would burn in the moonlight, varying only in degrees of burns and shades of bright red.

Merril had taken Doran to raise as his own son. Until his decision to leave Aidan out of the family business, he had always tried to treat them both the same (which as per the Keane family tradition largely inferred indifference toward them both). As Merril had continued to lose his own wits however, his own hostility deepened and grew into fits of rage. It was during one such breakdown that he had determined that it would be Aidan, the smarter of the two boys, who would break the chain of despair that had been his burden. Through Aidan, Merril would do all that he himself had lacked the courage or opportunity to accomplish.

Doran had understood as it had been explained to him by his father that as Aidan was the smarter of the two, that it would be Aidan who would get the opportunities in life. It would be Doran's calling to support his brother through his labor as he ascended. To Doran, this was a great honor. He knew that Aidan had always been the smart one, able to pick up new things in an instant. He also knew that he was not smart like that. And he loved his younger brother more than anything. He liked the idea that his work would be helping to support someone that he cared about so much. He felt very grown up to be contributing something to his family, especially for Aidan.

It had never been uncommon for their parents to up and disappear for a couple days at a stretch on a drunk somewhere. As long as Doran could remember, they had been there one day and gone the next and it had fallen upon his own shoulders to care for his little brother, to comfort him, and watch over him like the parents they never really had.

Doran had been inside the kitchen looking out the back window that night. He saw his father strike his mother to the ground and he watched as he beat Aidan with the buggy whip. Doran had wanted more than anything to shoot him that minute for hurting Aidan that way. Aidan had never harmed anyone. He was the kindest, gentlest boy that Doran could imagine. At the same time he was perplexed by what he had witnessed. With the exception of the time the two had broken the stained glass window in the entry door, he hadn't known his father to strike either one of them. Sure, sometimes when their parents drank they'd beat on each other, but both the boys knew to stay well hidden away when they were drunk and on the scrap like that.

It was often during those times that the two would just light out for a night or more. They never told their folks where they had gone, and for their own part, they had never asked either. But most nights, secretly, they'd sneak off and go stay with their grandpa Collin. Their pa had always said he'd lost his damned mind. He was right about that of course, but Grandpa Collin was always so happy to see the boys. He called them by the names of pa's long dead brothers, but it made him happy and he doted over the boys and fed and cared for them, so there had been no harm in it.

When Merril finally came back from the barn that night he was carrying a bottle and taking extra long pulls off of it. Doran could tell just by looking at him that he was upset. He yelled at his wife to put the boy to bed without his supper first then turned his full attention toward his bottle. Shortly after he saw to it that Aidan was in bed, he began to call for Doran. But Doran stayed hid until he heard him shout to his mother that, "the damned boy must've run off again."

Upon hearing that, Doran crawled up from the root cellar onto the back porch. He knew it was safe to come up that way because he could hear his parents talking on the front porch and the creaking of the porch swing. That meant they were sitting out there drinking again and would be for quite some time. Doran slid into the kitchen and grabbed the plate with half a chicken left on it. It was the remnants from the early supper they'd been eating when Aidan first rushed in. Then he slipped quietly out the back door making sure not to let the screen slam behind him. From there he pulled himself up the trellis to the small porch roof landing right outside their bedroom window.

The boys had developed the stealth of wildcats when it came to scurrying in and out of that window, but Doran admired himself on a whole new level for having made the ascent while balancing a plate of chicken. He hadn't made a noise nor dropped a crumb for the critters when he made his way into the window.

"Aidan?" He whispered to the figure that lay curled up into a tight ball in the bed with his back to the window. "Aidan...you awake?"

Aidan sniffled and sat up in the bed, "Yeah, I'm awake. Where's Papa at?"

"He's out in the swing with ma pulling on the bottle again. It's alright little brother. You sit up here and eat some chicken," he said, sitting on the bed beside his little brother and holding out the plate toward him.

"You had better scram, Doran. If Papa catches you in here, he'll..."

"You let me worry about him," Doran said, "besides, if he lays hand on my brother like that again, he had ought to be more worried about me anyways. I thought real hard about just shootin' him, but I thought I'd better see what it is you done first, just in case you might have had it comin' to ya."

"I did have it comin' Doran," Aidan began to cry again, "I let him down today at school." Aidan began to cry uncontrollably.

"Calm down little brother. You calm down. Just tell me what happened will you?" Doran said, wiping the tears off his brother's cheek.

Aidan told him the whole story, from the nun that morning and the yellow shirt and the big stone doorway and the giant doors. He told his brother about the kids in the changing room and the beating he got there and getting hit with the stick and beat with the paddle and all the kids sitting there laughing at him. He told him about after school when he just wanted to get home too, and how he pushed the kid and ran like hell only to get home to Pa. He told him how he had let their father down because he had been counting on him to make things right for the whole family. And he told Doran how sorry he was for letting him down because he was a Keane too, and he reckoned he'd let all of them down that day. Then he just sort of laid back and ate the chicken off the bone as tears fell down his cheeks the whole time.

After listening to the story, Doran sat quietly thinking for a while and then said succinctly, "Well that's just ass dumb. You didn't let anybody down little brother and don't you go on thinkin' it neither."

"You think so Doran, really?" Aidan's eyes lit up.

"I know so little brother. It aint your call to go get beat up by every damned body in stinkin' Melrose because Pa is afraid of em'. That's just ass dumb I tell ya." He replied.

"What am I gonna do Doran?" Aidan asked.

"Well, we could run away tonight and go and live with Grandpa Collin I reckon," Doran said thoughtfully.

"That's ass dumb too. Pa would find us there first thing he went to the dump. Besides, Grandpa Collin is crazy as a wild mule," Aidan replied.

"I reckon you're right little brother. Say, we could run off and jump on a train. Maybe we could get us a job with one of them circuses or something. Maybe even one of them wild west shows!" Doran said enthusiastically.

"Nah, we're just kids Doran. They'd never give us jobs. Besides, they'd probably arrest us first stop for being kids with no folks and all," Aidan replied.

"I've got it!" Doran exclaimed.

"Shhhhhhh!" Aidan replied, "Papa will hear you for sure!"

"I know just what to do little brother," Doran said proudly, "Here's what we'll do. Tomorrow, you just stay clear of everybody in the morning by getting to that school nice and early. Then during the day you stay out of that changing room and if you got to go piss you just go in your britches, you understand me? Then after school here's what we'll do..." Aidan listened intently as Doran laid out the rest of the plan.

It was a terrible plan of course. Even little Aidan knew it was a terrible plan and Doran knew for absolute certain that it was a terrible plan, but he was the big brother after all and if he couldn't be counted on to do *something,* then what good was he anyways? If there was ever a time that they needed a father or a real mother, Doran had thought to himself, it's now. But they had neither. They only had each other and they both knew it.

After finishing the chicken and hearing Doran's plan in its entirety, Aidan finally managed a tiny smile that evening. He looked at Doran and curled his lips upward as if to say thank you, I love you, I need you, you have saved my life, and then he collapsed back onto the bed and slept the sleep of the dead. That night he would not toss, nor turn, nor miss a wink. Doran on the other hand would not see the backside of his own eyelids at all. He was worried enough for both of them anyways. It really was a terrible plan...

Chapter 13   Vengeance

That morning began much the same as the last except that by the time Aidan got out of bed, his father and brother had already gone off to the dump to begin their work day. His mother called him down and had cooked some oats for him. He had always hated oats, but his mother had a way of doctoring them up so they were somewhat sweet and at least edible.

"How are you feeling today my little angel?" She inquired, coaxing a contorted smile from his otherwise miserable, gloomy face.

"Fine," he replied. He could tell by her look and tone that she had drank too much the night before. She and papa *always* drank too much.

"You know, your father only wants what is best for you Aidan. He..." She looked toward the floor. She always looked at the floor when she was making excuses for Papa.

"I know," he interrupted, "I'll try harder to make him proud of me mama. I promise." She had always made excuses for him the day after a drunk. No matter what he had done, no matter how awful things had been between them the night before. She could be trying to take his head clean off with a whiskey bottle the night before because he had hit her again, and the next morning she'd be standing there saying how father knows best and how much he cared about us all. But today, he didn't feel much like hearing it. So after quickly devouring his oats Aidan trotted out the door and off to school.

He had done just as Doran had told him to. He had arrived at the school almost a full hour before class was set to begin. He was there when the cleaning man came and opened the big front double doors. Indeed, he had been correct too, for the cleaning man must have stood almost 6' tall and weighed over 200 pounds! He was the biggest man that Aidan had ever seen.

After the doors opened and the cleaning man disappeared back into the depths of the building, Aidan ran inside and quietly made his way past the office door where he could hear the nuns inside talking and laughing. He skulked his way on down the hallway to the door marked with a large number four and he ducked inside.

Aidan paused as he got inside the classroom and pondered on the rows of empty desks. He had never been in a classroom before, but it seemed to him that one should not simply walk into a room full of chairs and pick the one nearest the door...unless of course he felt like he might have to go to the outhouse a lot that day. But Aidan wouldn't be going to the outhouse or the changing room that day, maybe never again even. Finally, he settled on a desk in about the middle of the group. It was not too close to the front for him to be noticed much, yet not too far to the back so that he appeared to be trying to hide. There really was a lot to consider in such a decision.

The young nun that walked into the room looked at Aidan and gave a tiny smile. "Hello," she'd said, "My name is Sister Catherine."

"I'm Aidan," he said sheepishly.

"Well Aidan," she replied, "I have you a seat already assigned right over there." Sister Catherine pointed toward the windows that lined the wall furthest from the door.

Aidan's eyes followed her pointing finger to a lone chair that sat against the wall. It wasn't even a desk, just an old wooden chair sitting all by itself outside of the neatly aligned rows of desks. He looked back at Sister Catherine.

"We do not allow yellow shirted students to sit with the rest until they have taken communion," she explained. "Then you will be able to sit with everyone else and wear the crimson shirts too." She smiled brightly and had interjected excitement into her tone.

Aidan would find that whenever she talked to him about receiving communion her enthusiasm and mannerism would remind him of the traveling salesman who came around a few times a year and tried to sell stuff to papa.

"Buy one of these today and you'll get this one for free!" He'd say smiling with the exact same tone that Sister Catherine used.

"Take communion today, and we'll throw in a crimson shirt AND you'll get to sit with these wonderful kids over here!" He imagined her saying.

Aidan took his seat against the wall just as the other children began shuffling in. His first day they had all looked like a bunch of rich city fancies in their matching crimson shirts, but they looked very different to him now. He looked closer at them and saw that this one had holes in his shoes that you could put your whole fist through, but they'd been stuffed with cardboard. And that one had pants that had been sewn out of flour bags. Aidan's mother had an apron that had been sewn out of flower bags and his grandpa had an undershirt, but he'd never seen flour bag pants before. Papa had been right all along, he thought. These ones were no better than him at all if you took away their fancy crimson shirts.

The other boys in the class all took turns staring at Aidan that day. Some would glare in contempt. He could feel the hatred burning holes in him from these boys. Others would look at their shoes when he caught them staring. Others still would look at him with a curious wonder, like he was a caged animal that they'd never laid eyes on before.

Some of them even gave a half smile every now and then as if to say that they understood because they were friendless loners too. But they were quick to look away too because no matter how low they had descended on the social pecking order, Aidan sitting alone in his yellow shirt was a reminder that things could always get worse. Even the loneliest friendless child in the whole school would never put a target on their own backs by trying to befriend him. By his presence alone, though, all the rest of them got to move up one notch because they weren't him. Will everyone who is not wearing a yellow shirt please take one step backwards?

Aidan did not go to the changing room that day. He didn't go outside to use the privy either. He didn't even go to lunch. He just sat there in his seat the entire day. Still, it had been a good day. No one had beaten him up that day AND he hadn't seen the Reverend Mother either. Sure, he had been hit three times by Sister Catherine with something that looked like a riding crop, but those had all been because he was falling asleep. What made it even better was that she had hit four other boys with the thing that day as well so for once, Aidan was not alone. He enjoyed feeling like a part of a crowd, even if only in their shared pain and the telling red welts on their arms and the backs of their necks.

That afternoon when school finally let out, Aidan hung around as long as he could after class. He was hoping that on this day at least, that he could come early enough, and leave late enough, to avoid another beating or confrontation with anyone. But eventually Sister Catherine had looked up from her desk and the mountain of papers she had been checking and shooed him along.

Entering the hallways he found them empty save a stray nun here and there. Passing through the big doorway, he peered outside the building and saw the last few boys playing as they walked out of the school yard. They were going the opposite direction as him any-ways. It was all clear! He ran across the school yard and into the road. He ran at a slow pace carrying his things as he went. One block was behind him already. He could see the tree line up ahead!

Just then, he heard the boys all screaming like wild Indians as they ran toward the old dirt road. They had been hiding behind a chicken shed, laying in wait to finish off the yellow shirt that had left them the day before with egg on their face. Aidan dropped his things in the road and ran with all the might that his seven year old legs could muster. If only he could make it to the trees, everything would be alright.

Earlier that morning when Doran had arrived at the dump with Papa, he'd worked twice as hard as he ever had before. For every chunk of cast iron that he found and took back to their cart for his Pa to see, he found another one and stashed it away on the far side of the mound. What had begun years ago as a ditch where folks started throwing an item or two had turned into a mile long mountain range of junk. If there had ever been a ditch there under the mountain, Doran couldn't tell it. By then it was large enough for a boy to get lost for a few hours so long as he had a pile of goods to show for the time.

Doran had squirreled away loot all morning and then went about looking until he found him a nice stout axe handle. The head end had been broken off, but it would do the job quite well, he thought.

Round about three o'clock, Doran had disappeared over a small crest with his axe handle and high tailed it for town. He had got there just in time to hide himself and catch his breath. He stowed away behind a huge old fallen log and listened.

There it was! He heard the sound of footsteps running like mad down the road. In the distance but closing fast he could hear the wild screams of the other boys. As the first set of footsteps were upon him, he grabbed his axe handle and leaped out into the trailhead. Doran had slightly misjudged the distance of the footsteps though, and he and Aidan nearly knocked each other over. Aidan stopped and turned and stood his ground as the four boys slowed on their approach.

"You leave my brother alone, you bastards!" Doran screamed at the boys who had slowed to a walk but continued to move toward them. "Aidan, you run home! Run!"

Aidan stood still. "No Doran. I'm standing my ground. I'm not letting pa down any more."

"What? Run home now Aidan!" Doran yelled as the boys closed in.

"No! I ain't running from no chicken shit Catholic sons of whores any more!" Aidan replied.

Doran looked at his brother and gave the tiniest faint hint of a smile out of the corner of his mouth. Their father might never be proud of him, but by God, Doran was. "Well, okay then little brother," he said.

With that Doran stepped toward the biggest boy and the one who moved at the front of the pack. He drew back the axe handle and swung it with all of his might. He aimed to kill the boy for torturing his little brother. He'd beat all of them within an inch of their lives and come back and beat them again if that's what it took. His eyes filled with rage, his heart pounded almost out of his chest. He let loose a crazy scream as the axe handle swung forward. Just then, within the tiniest fraction of a fraction of a second before the handle struck the boy in the head and lay him low to the ground, it slipped. It just slipped.

Doran watched in horror as the thing slipped from his ten year old grip. So much of what they sorted through at that old dump was covered in grease. It'd never even occurred to him that he had inadvertently applied a slick greasy coating to the thing as he carried it around with him throughout the day. But there it went. Doran watched with wide, astonished eyes as the handle flew through the air and bounced into the road. Then he looked back at Aidan with confusion and astonishment. "Shit," he mouthed under his breath.

Just like that, the boys were upon them like a wolf pack. Doran fought a good fight, but there were two of them, both a little older than him, and they soon had him on the ground. Aidan on the other hand only stood there and waited for the beating to come. Once they were upon him striking his face and head, he fell to the ground and curled into his protective ball, crying for them to stop, and waiting for it to end. Finally, the boys tired of beating them, gave them a final kick to the ribs, and walked away, yelling taunts back at the two brothers.

The two collected themselves and slowly got to their feet. Aidan had a freshly bloodied lip and violet welt above his swelling eye. Doran had the worst of it with what appeared to a broken nose that bled like a winter hog with its throat cut. The two walked silently toward home down the trail, limping and rubbing their various injuries.

"You should have run," Doran finally said, breaking the silence.

"Yeah," Aidan replied.

"I've been thinking," Doran said, "that tomorrow you ought to do everything I told you to today, but just take a different way home."

"Good idea," Aidan said thoughtfully.

"That really was a terrible idea," Doran said smiling through his bloodstained front teeth.

"It sure was," Aidan replied, and the two broken toy soldiers laughed the rest of the way home.

Chapter 14   Bibs

Aidan followed Doran's plan every day and most days, it served him well. He'd survived to see his eleventh birthday anyways. There were good days when he might only receive a swat or two from Sister Catherine. But there were plenty of bad days too, when one way or another, some group of boys would catch up with him and bloody his yellow shirt. Of course, there were far worse days than those even, like when the Reverend Mother would be in a particularly foul state and she'd seek him out, finding something to beat and humiliate him for. The worst days of all though, were when Pa had been drinking and decided to help "toughen him up" with another brutal beating. Pa's beatings were always the worst because they lasted the longest, hurt the most, and because they were from Pa.

It had worked though, because come hell or high water, Aidan never cried from pain any more. He'd stand his ground and take his beating no matter what. Nobody could take a beating like Aidan. But he did still cry. Doran heard it all the time. Late at night, after they'd gone to bed he could hear Aidan weeping. He had stopped going to his bed to try to comfort him because mostly, it just upset him to know that someone could hear him crying, even Doran. So Doran tried to leave him his pride and just didn't say anything, but it always bothered him and always, he had to stop himself from going to Aidan's bed to comfort him.

Some days if Doran could get away, he'd meet Aidan in town and walk home with him. Aidan must've had a hundred different ways home by then, so he'd have to go wait right outside the school if he wanted to catch him. But Doran couldn't always get away from the dump, so more often than not, Aidan was on his own. Still, they never tried to go to town with an axe handle or anything like that again. That WAS a terrible idea. Even if it had worked they'd be in jail or dead after being hanged by a thousand angry Catholics. Still, sometimes the two fought together side by side, but they always lost of course, because Aidan would never hit them back. Doran would swing like crazy, but Aidan would just stand there and let them pummel him.

It was a few days after Aidan's eleventh birthday and Doran waited outside the school building as the crimson shirts emerged into the sunlight and disappeared. Finally, Aidan walked outside and headed for the road. Doran ran to catch up and fell in beside his brother.

"Hey," Aidan said quietly. It had been a bad day. Doran could always tell when Aidan had a particularly bad day at the school just by the tone of his voice.

"Reverend Mother?" Doran inquired.

"Yeah," Aidan replied.

"That no good whore," Doran said, shaking his head and grimacing.

"Shhhh," said Aidan, "they'll hear you."

"They can't hear me way out here on the road. No good whore!" He shouted.

"They can hear everything, Doran," Aidan said quietly, "You don't understand."

"Where you going?" Doran asked, realizing they were headed the opposite direction of home.

"Home," Aidan replied dryly, "It's a shortcut I know."

"Oh great," Doran said and continued walking. His brother had made it an art form out of finding new routes home. Often times, however, his "shortcuts" might be two or even three MILES out of the way. Doran figured that it served the dual purpose of avoiding the roving groups of boys in Melrose, and taking longer to get home. Aidan didn't like going home much any more.

"It's an awful nice day out," Doran said, "I thought we might sneak over to the McDougal place this evening and do some fishing. One last time before the snow falls. What do you say?"

"Sure," Aidan answered. McDougal hated *anyone* trespassing on his property, especially the heathenish Keane boys. He had even run them off once and then showed up at the house to complain to their father. But Pa had been drinking that day and he called McDougal all sorts of names and threatened to kill him if he ever set foot on his place again. Since then McDougal carried a shotgun with him everywhere he went loaded with rock salt shells. They wouldn't kill you, but the rock salt made a wound and then melted inside of it, burning like crazy until it healed. But still, Doran liked that the old man hated them trespassing, so he took great pride and joy in every fish that they could steal out of his pond.

As they walked along the old dirt road, about a mile outside of town, they passed a large white two story house. It had all the fancy scrolled woodwork on the eaves and along the porch that signified a doctor or somebody important. The house and even the outbuildings had a fresh coat of whitewash on them. Aside from one or two houses in Melrose, it was the nicest home they had ever set eyes on.

They were so busy admiring the home as they walked that they hadn't noticed the head sticking up in the weeds along the roadside ditch. Just then the head emerged and threw a rock at them.

"Hey! You there, boy! What are you doin' on my road?" The girl had missed their heads with the rock she had thrown, but that didn't stop both of them giving a loud fright and nearly jumping out of their shoes.

"Hey, I'm talking to you!" She yelled at them as they continued to walk on by her.

Aidan turned and looked at her over his shoulder as they passed. She was wearing dirty grey bibs. You could tell if you looked at them real close that they used to be colorful, but they were so faded and dirty that they just appeared to be a mottled dark grey.

The little girl herself, probably around his own age, he thought, had a strawberry golden head of hair that must've had a thousand little curls in it. Her face was covered in patches of dirt like she'd been sitting in the ditch eating mud pies, but her eyes shone bright green in the afternoon sun. And even while she yelled at them in a nasty tone, she had a smile on her face that warmed his heart and made him want to smile right back at her.

"What's your name boy?" She called after them, looking Aidan in the eye.

Aidan stopped and turned and looked at her. "Aidan," he said.

"Come on little brother," Doran said, grabbing his arm and pulling him on down the road, "that girl is crazy."

"Well, you best stay off my road, Aidan!" She called after them, "If'n you know what's best for ya!"

Just then a portly woman in a blue dress and a huge white apron emerged from the porch and yelled out to the girl as she beat tracks across the lawn to get to her. "Maizey May," the woman cried, "You get in here girl!"

"Bye," the curly haired girl in the dirty bibs with the dirt covered face smiled bigger than she had before and maybe even bigger than Aidan had ever seen anyone smile, just as the old woman snatched her by the arm and drug her toward the house.

"What's the matter with you, girl," he heard the woman say, but she had turned away from them and he couldn't hear what else she was saying, only that she kept yelling at the girl all the way back to the house.

"Well, I never," Doran said, feigning outrage, "I hope that girl gets a good whoopin' for acting that way!"

"Yeah," Aidan said.

The rest of the way home and all that night fishing, Doran talked and talked. He always talked a lot when he was in a particularly good mood. He also always talked a lot when Aidan was in a particularly bad mood or had a particularly bad day. Aidan knew that his brother thought that he was being quiet because he'd had a bad day. Fact was, he did have a bad day. But that wasn't why he was being quiet. Ever since he had laid eyes on her, he couldn't get that smile out of his head. Or that dirty face, or those tiny locks of strawberry and gold hair. He never thought too much of girls, but he couldn't stop thinking about this one. He'd never seen a smile like that one before in his whole entire life.

Chapter 15   The Long Way Home

Ever since the day he saw the sparkly eyed little dirty faced girl, Aidan could not get her out of his mind. Her house, or what he assumed to be her house, was on a road that took Aidan almost three miles out of his way to get home. Every day he walked on his favorite new "short cut" but as the days grew colder and shorter his hopes of ever seeing her again began to fade.

What's worse was the other boys had caught onto him. They knew which way he went now, which made it easier for them to lay in wait. When his brother was with him, they'd usually let them pass, but whenever he was alone, they'd taunt him and shove him around at the very least. Among the boys of Melrose, it became a right of passage to beat up the yellow shirt. If a kid appeared to be scared of most things, the other boys might taunt him calling him a chicken. They'd say that he was even too scared to fight the yellow shirt and HE is scared of everything, they'd say. Finally, amidst the endless taunts, another boy would lay in wait with the regulars and take his own reluctant turn at beating up Aidan.

Even as he lay curled in his protective ball, absorbing blows to the head and ribs, he would think of Maizey May. If he thought about her smile and her beautiful green eyes shining at him, he could block all of the pain out of his head. So that is what he did. With each round of beatings, each assault by the Reverend Mother, each pummeling from his father, he would drift away to a quiet and peaceful place in his mind where it was only him and the smiling, dirty faced little girl in her grey bibs.

His 'shortcut' made for many a long and lonely walk home, especially in the colder winter months. As the deep snows set in, he
knew that there was almost no chance of getting to see her, but still,
he braved the cold and the snow and the wind and walked the extra
miles. He would pass the big white house and squint to see through
the laced curtain as he passed in the hopes that he might catch but a
glimpse of her silhouette. He never did see her of course. The house
itself set too far off the road for that. But it never stopped him from
walking so far out of the way.

It didn't faze him that he received extra beatings in his bid to see her
again. She was only a dirty faced little girl, but to him she had
become an angel; a real honest to goodness angel. She would swoop
down from the heavens whenever he was being hurt and take him
away from it all. He was too young to care much about girls yet,
save one. She was all that he could think about while he was awake
and all that he dreamed of while he slept. To him, she was everything.

It was late January of 1928. The wind howled as Aidan made his
way down the dirt road that led out of town and eventually led past
Maizey's house. When he had left school he began to see giant
snowflakes falling all about him. There wasn't a lot of snow at that
time, but the strong winds blew the same flakes back into the air
even before they hit the ground. Then they would wind around and
hit him sideways. Aidan was certain that he'd been slammed in the
face by the same snowflake three times as it made its winding
journey to the ground.

By the time he had reached the edge of town he turned to look
behind him. From that vantage point in the road, he could usually
see most of the town as it sprawled northward up the hill and out of
the small Melrose valley. On that day however, he could see nothing
but white snow blowing about. As he trudged on he leaned into the
wind and held his scarf over his face to keep the stinging wet snow
from slamming into his tender, rosy, wind burnt cheeks.

There would be no Catholic boys skulking about waiting to give him
a beating in the road that day. In fact, as he carried on he couldn't
even see the road. He had no idea where he was or how far he had

gone. Twice, he even found himself walking into the ditch that ran alongside the road, having inadvertently lost his bearings and wandered off the road itself.

As the snow piled up and the wind continued to howl, walking became more and more difficult. There were times when the wind would shift unexpectedly and steal his breath away for a moment. Still he struggled on. Finally, he made the fateful decision to leave the road and try to travel cross country to the West. It would be risky sure enough, but the road was doing him less and less good anyhow. If it continued to worsen, he would soon not be able to tell road from pasture.

Turning to the west and leaving the road, the wind picked up steam. In an instant it seemed to have increased to twice the speed it had been just moments before. He turned to look for the road behind him and it was completely gone, disappeared in a blinding white haze. He turned back around and all of a sudden realized that he hadn't even a clue about which direction he was facing any more. He began to panic. His heart began to race, but he knew that the wind had been out of the northwest so he struggled to keep his face into the wind with it slightly bared more upon his right cheek.

Visibility was all but gone. As the day gave way to darkness, he could no loner see even his own feet and he felt his eye lashes begin to ice up. Each time he blinked or was struck in the eye with wet snow, it became increasingly difficult to get them open again. This was it, he thought. He was out of breath, his eyes were failing, and it was getting darker by the minute. He was going to die and he knew it.

It seemed like every year there were stories about some kid in Southern Iowa getting caught in a snowstorm and freezing to death. During the worst of blizzards there was always someone getting lost on their way to their own barn or even the outhouse and not being found until the next morning. They almost always took their clothes off before they died though, he'd heard. Almost all of them took their clothes off is what his Pa had said, who had helped find two Methodists a few years back who'd been caught in a storm.

They must've given up and prepared to die, Aidan had thought. He began to consider that perhaps he should do the same and just end it right then and there. But even as the thought occurred to him and he was accepting his death and thinking about his brother and what would become of him, he slammed his head into something.

"Ooooow. Damnit!" He screamed and began to cry. Not from the pain. He could take any pain in the world now. It was because he had only wanted to see HER one more time before he died. Now, not only was that never going to happen again, he was going to die out there. Worse yet, he was going to die in a God damned yellow shirt. As if all of that wasn't bad enough, God thought it would be funny to have him run into a few things with his damned head before he finished him off too!

He reached out with his hand to figure out how big the tree was he needed to get around. His hand revealed a smooth surface though that wasn't a tree at all. It kept going too. It had to be a building. Maybe a home or...a barn! It was a barn! He walked around the building feeling it with his hands until he came to the groove that marked a door. Then he felt up and down both sides of the thing until he finally found a handle. He opened it and entered the old barn. Slamming it behind him, he was in complete darkness. He collapsed with his back against the door and took his hat and scarf off.

He was exhausted. Aidan had never been so tired in his entire life. He didn't want to move. He was too tired to even get up and too tired to try. Reaching over to the stall just inside the door, he pulled out a small pile of straw. With every bit of strength that remained in his body, he piled the straw around his legs and spread it over his chest. Then he put his hat back on his head, pulling it down tight, bundled up in his scarf and simply let himself fall asleep. He dreamed of her again.

Chapter 16   Sweet Dreams

As Aidan slept he saw her once again. This time she had been running through an open meadow. Her bibs were bright and new and her face was clean and pure as the freshly fallen snow. He tried to catch her, but the tall grass kept binding around his legs. She had no such difficulty however and continued to run just out of his grasp. Then she would stop and tease him by running small circles around him. He followed her with his eyes and head until his neck could not turn anymore, then he would quickly turn his head the other way to keep watching her.

Maizey's tiny curls blew in the gentle wind behind her as she ran. It shone a bright yellow in the afternoon sun and glimmered and sparkled like Papa's gold watch. And her smile, oh that smile of hers. It lit up his whole world and warmed him to the bone. She had the most amazing smile he had ever seen. Every time she smiled her beautiful green eyes lit up and Aidan felt at home. Not like being at home with his father and mother and Doran either, but a place called home in his heart that he had never even really been before.

"Aidan?" she cried.

"Oh Maizey," he said to her smiling, as she ran about him in the field laughing and brushing her hand over the tall wild flowers.

"How did you know my name?" She said.

"Maizey," he said again smiling.

72

"Aidan!" she yelled and as she did the meadow grew very cold.

Aidan looked into her green eyes and they had lost their shine. Her golden hair was covered in a thick knitted hat. She wasn't laughing any more either. She wasn't even smiling.

"Aidan. Are you alright? What are you doing?" she asked.

Aidan rubbed his eyes and pulled the hay off of his lap, stretching his arms and aching back. Suddenly it hit him. He remembered the snowstorm and the barn and the hay and, oh God! It really was her. But how could it be her? He sat up and scrambled backwards against the barn door. As he did, it flew open and he fell backwards again only to find himself lying in the snow blinded by the brightness. The blinding rays of the early morning sun shone down in his eyes until everything grew dark as if an eclipse was suddenly upon him.

"What's this?" The man's voice said sharply. "What are you doing out here in my barn, boy?"

Aidan's eyes focused and adjusted to the light. As they did, the figure of a man standing over him came into view. He was a large man with a full dark beard and a thick moustache. He didn't appear to be as angry as he was perplexed.

"I, I was lost in the storm, sir. I couldn't find my way home from school. Then I sort of ran into this here barn." Aidan said, still lying in the snow on his back looking up at the figure.

"I thought Aidan might be dead, Daddy," Maizey spoke. Her voice was so soft and heavenly to his ears. He thought that even this must certainly be a dream. He even reckoned himself to be really still lying in the road somewhere without any clothes on, dying in the storm.

Maizey's father grabbed him up by the shoulder of the coat and brought him directly to his feet. "You know this boy, Maizey May?" he asked.

73

"Yes sir," she replied, "he's a friend of mine. Aidan and I play sometimes out along the road. Don't we Aidan?" She smiled at him.

"Uh, yes sir, that's right," Aidan replied, going along with her lie. He didn't care much for lying, especially to Maizey's father who he'd just met. Not to say he didn't lie to the nuns all the time. Hell, they had it coming treating folks the way they did. But this was some adult he didn't even really know yet. He didn't like it at all, but he thought that it might be best, given the circumstances, just to go along with her.

"And you spent the whole night in this here barn son?" He asked.

"Yes sir." Aidan replied, still trying to get his balance from being woken up and dragged to his feet all in the matter of less than a minute.

"We best get you in the house then so you can warm yourself, I reckon. You must be half frozen, boy. Not to mention starved to death! Maizey, you run on upstairs and tell your Ma to come down and make some breakfast for this lad," he ordered.

"Yes, Pa," she said, giving Aidan one final huge knowing smile before she turned away. Aidan watched her go, half running and half skipping all the way to the back porch of the house.

"You should have come to the house last night boy," the man said, "You might have frozen clean to death out here."

"I couldn't see the house, sir. I couldn't even see this barn even. Just sort of ran into it really." Aidan replied.

"Well, you come with me lad, we'll get you straightened out," he said, leading the way toward the big house. "You're lucky to be alive. I bet your folks must be sick with worry."

As they neared the back door, Aidan grew restless and nervous and even thought of turning and running away, but he knew that somewhere inside was Maizey May. He simply couldn't resist the urge to see her once again through eyes not still clouded with sleep and cold. As her father opened the door and stepped across the threshold, Aidan paused to inspect the fancy scroll work in the wood that seemed to line every window and eave and even the railings on the porch.

He ran his hand over the small wooden rail that led up the few stairs to the back porch. It was in the shape of some sort of woman's bust, maybe a mermaid, he thought. It was difficult to tell with everything half covered in ice and snow and all. He had never been anywhere or stood so close to anything so fancy in all his life. It made him even more nervous.

"It was my uncle's house," her father said from inside the doorway. He had stopped to find the boy admiring the woodwork. "He was a ship's carver in Ireland. He came here forty years ago and built this house with his own two hands. He'd married well and done it all with the dowry he'd received. He's long gone now, but he left it to us so we came here some years ago from Ohio country," he said with the thoughtful look upon his face of a man remembering things of long ago. He wasn't looking at Aidan, but somewhere above him over his left shoulder as if reading a story book that hovered somewhere in the air behind him. "Anyhow, get on inside boy!"

Aidan stepped inside and followed the man through the interior door that led to the kitchen. You could see that once it had been a grand kitchen with a huge dining hall on past, inside the house. Now it was mostly empty, devoid of the many fancy things that would have once filled such grand rooms. There was only a small wooden table in the middle of the dining hall with chairs enough for four.

In the kitchen, there was but a small wood cook stove in the middle of the room with stumps around it that served as stools. In the corner of the room a splitting maul leaned against the wall. Aidan correctly reckoned that on cold winter nights, the maul found better use of the stump chairs in the fire.

The paint on all the trim was split and cracking and falling in chunks to the floor. The paper, where there was paper on the walls was torn and stained in the places where smoke and stove heat had caused it damage.

"Have a seat," the man said. "I've done my best to keep up the outside like he had it. But we've had to sell most of his things in here just to keep us going."

Aidan sat on one of the stumps and began to remove his clothes to let the heat from the stove permeate his frozen bones.

"I am Fergus," he said, "Fergus Mullan." He put out his hand and Aidan shook it firmly as he might with his frozen hand.

"I am Aidan Keane," he replied.

Just then Maizey entered the kitchen with her mother in tow. She smiled and glanced at him out of the corner of her eye as she pretended to turn toward the cupboards without looking.

"Hello young man," her mother said. "I understand you're about half starved to death.

"Oh. No ma'am. I'm just getting warmed up and I will be on my way home again," he said, "You needn't..."

"Nonsense," the woman replied smiling warmly, "tis no trouble at all, lad."

Maizey had opened a drawer and produced a bundle of white clothe. Turning back, she handed it to her mother. As the large woman had unwound the bundle, there appeared four biscuits which she placed on a plate. Using the cloth, she then opened the warming oven above the stove and slid them inside. Next, she removed one of the stove lids and the flames leapt out of the small circular opening. Maizey handed her a small but thick cast iron skillet and she placed it over the open hole.

Aidan's stomach growled as he smelled the salted pork beginning to cook. Within a minute, it had filled the entire room with a magnificent odor that penetrated the nostrils and watered the mouth. You really could almost taste the salt and pork in the air while it cooked, he remembered thinking.

Maizey stood to the rear of her mother and behind her father who sat near the stove on a stump as well. She just stood there smiling at Aidan. He tried not to appear to her parents to be staring at her, but his eyes betrayed him and kept being draw to hers. They were wonderful eyes. Green and sparkly like emeralds and her smile was even warmer than he had remembered it.

Every time he looked at her, her smile would grow almost impercep- tibly larger and her cheeks would flush two shades of darker pink. She had wonderful skin, he had thought to himself. It was light like Doran's almost, but without the blemishes and pasty paleness of a full redhead like his brother. It flushed in the most incredible shades of red and pink too.

"Keane, eh boy?" Fergus had been sitting, thinking quietly since his wife and daughter had walked in. He had taken advantage of the moment to light his pipe and relax from his outside chores. Emerg- ing from his thoughtful introspective trance, he found the boy staring with open, drooling jowls at his only daughter. To him, they seemed too young for any such nonsense, but he still thought it best to intervene in the stare-off nonetheless.

"I'm sorry sir, what?" Aidan replied, turning to her father with a confused and embarrassed look. He knew he had been caught. It was hard enough just to look into a girl's eyes like that. Normally, he'd be too shy and embarrassed to do it, but it was *her,* his angel. Having someone else catch him in the act though, particularly her Father, caused his own face to flush a beat red. Turning to him, he could feel every drop of blood in his body rush to his face.

"I say you're a Keane, is that right lad?" He repeated.

"Oh, yes sir. That's correct," he said. As he answered, Maizey's mother took the biscuit plate out of the warming oven. Next she slid the salted pork onto it and handed it to him.

"Thank you, Ma'am," he said as he placed a piece of salted pork on his tongue and let it absorb the salt off of it before he began to chew.

"No mention of it lad," she replied.

"Are you any relation to Joseph Keane?" her father finally asked.

"No sir, not that I'm aware of," Aidan replied as he downed a biscuit. They were magnificent. They were moist and flaky and penetrated through and through with rich butter. Not the stout sour butter like his parents made either. It was the sweet, salty, creamy sort of butter that you could eat all by itself, if you had a notion to.

"What about Carrig Keane? You've the look of old Carrig to you. Is he your Pa then?" he asked with a bit of a smile of recognition, shaking his head in slow affirmation.

"No sir," Aidan replied amidst swallowing another biscuit almost whole, "My Pa is Merril Keane."

"I guess that I don't know him," said Fergus, looking a bit confused, but still thoughtful as he took another pull off of his pipe and scratched his beard.

Aidan popped the last bite of biscuit into his mouth and in so doing he felt the warmth of his full stomach spreading through his entire body. He handed his plate to Maizey's mother and thanked her as he removed his outer shirt. He was sitting too close to the stove, but he thought it best to warm every layer before bundling back up and heading for home.

Maizey's Father stood up and pulled the pipe from his mouth. His eyes widened as he came to some realization that he had yet to share. His mouth agape, he struggled for his words to catch up with his thoughts. Aidan panicked. The God damned yellow shirt! He realized suddenly that his yellow shirt had betrayed him.

"Here he is mother!" He shouted excitedly, "The one the good Reverend Father O'Malley warned us about that crawled out of the garbage to test the souls of the boys at the school! Remove yourself from this house of the Lord, heathen!" The large man screamed, pointing his pipe at Aidan.

Aidan threw his shirt back on and grabbed his pile of clothes while scrambling for the door. Damn this yellow shirt, he thought again. He hated those shirts. Stopping a few feet outside the door, he finished bundling back up. Then slowly, he headed out across the back yard toward the field behind the barn. Them Catholics sure do make good butter, he thought to himself.

However frightened or saddened he had been by her Father's rage, he could not help but feel upbeat for having seen Maizey again. He now had a hundred more images in his mind of her amazing eyes and her warm smile to fill his dreams anew. Visions of her filled his head as he waded through the deep snow drifts.

Those eyes he thought to himself, those God damned eyes! He could simply fall right into those eyes and never even want to come back out into this world again. They were emerald pools of warm joy like he'd never seen before. Over frozen creek bottoms and through briar patches, across open fields and thick stands of timber, she stayed with him. She would always be with him, he thought, *Always*.

Chapter 17   Boots

The warmth that Aidan had absorbed from the fire had been slowly losing ground as the cold worked its way back through his layers of clothes. Once again, it had penetrated his bones as he approached the dump. He hated the thought of stopping there without Doran, but as he saw smoke rising out of his grandfather's chimney, he thought it wise that he stop and warm himself again, lessen he freeze solid before he made it home.

He had been there a hundred times with his brother, but Aidan never dared go to the dump alone. His grandfather had lost his mind long before, he was told. To him he had always been crazy and Aidan was genuinely afraid of the old man. Besides, his father had banned him from going to the dump for any reason. He was always afraid that Aidan would like it there better than he liked going to school and learning, so he simply forbade him to ever go there. Aidan had been the hope of his Father for the future of the entire Keane Family. The redemption of all of them rested squarely upon his shoulders.

Aidan knocked on the awkwardly fashioned, ill fitting door of his grandfather's shanty house. He had made some ten odd shanties and only the smoke from the fire inside had betrayed him as to which one he was squirreled away in at the moment.

"What do you want, you bastards?!?!" The voice screamed from inside.

"It's me Grandpa!" he replied, "Aidan. Let me in. It's freezing out here!"

The door creaked open and his grandfather's head peered out from inside around the corner. Then the door opened all the way and he found that his grandfather was holding a shotgun.

"Innis, Get in here lad! What have you been doing out there in the cold, boy?" He said, smiling to reveal his toothless mouth. He always called him Innis. That had been the name of one of his elder sons who had passed long ago. He had always thought that Aidan and his brother were his long past sons. To the crazy old man, it was as if they weren't really gone at all, but had only just been out playing in the dump for years at a time and finally come home for supper.

His grandfather pulled him inside and threw shut the door behind him. Then he used a large iron bar to wedge the thing shut and leaned a long piece of wood against it with a bunch of cans and bottles tied to the top.

"There! That'll let me know when the bastards come for me again Innis! You best get in here by the stove lad! They're coming for us, Innis! They're coming for us alright. The bastards come last night. They've been stealing my things outside for years and I've only been able to cuss em'. But last night, in they came during the storm. I waited until he come into the other room there yonder and then Wham! I give it to him sure as anything! Right in the head I did with that chunk of iron. Drug him out back and threw him to the rats I did! They'll think again about coming to get ole Collin Keane I reckon sure enough." The old man flashed another toothless smile at him, and gave a quick wink. It was as if he had to try real hard to wink though, contorting every muscle in his face to pull it off.

He was babbling again, Aidan thought. But at least it was a good day. On a bad day when they visited, the old man couldn't even say a sentence, just cursed and yelled and screamed incoherently. Yes, today was a good day alright.

Aidan looked at the ceiling where the tin roof blew up and down with the wind. In that corner of what grandpa called a house the snow piled up inside. The stove burned hot and if you sat beside it, it'd keep you warm, but only on one side. The other side was cold as the outdoors itself. So you sat close to the stove and burnt the front of you while your back got colder, then you switched. It wasn't a great method of warming yourself, but it was better than nothing.

In the opposite corner of the snow pile, lay a huge pile of linens, furs, and blankets. It was Grandpa's bed. He could lie down in that huge stack of rags and cover up with thirty layers at night, waking the next morning with the stove completely out and not have frozen to death. It was just that thick. Aidan wondered how many rats must also call it their home as well.

"Well, grandpa," he said after burning his front and backside twice by the fire and still shivering, "I had better get going now."

"You be careful out there boy!" He said as he removed the blockade of debris from in front of the door. "They'll be coming for us I tell you. Once they see that we've killed one of their own, those kneeling bastards will all be coming for us!"

"Yes sir, Grandpa," he said as he made his way back outside into the comparatively fresh clean air of the trash dump. That's the thing about old people, he thought to himself, especially the crazy ones. They smell just God awful. And the crazier and older they are, the more God awful they smell!

As Aidan made his way over the small mountains of garbage, he imagined that 'they' were coming for them. He envisioned an army of Catholics, or *"kneelers"* as Grandpa called them, crawling up on the far side of the garbage pile and launching medieval catapults of flaming garbage on to grandpa's shack. He imagined his grandfather coming out blasting away with his shotgun and cursing and taking out a dozen Catholics before they finally overran him and killed him. Then he imagined the Reverend Mother scalping the old man and eating his still beating heart.

He was a little less scared by the funny old man after thinking of all that. Aidan actually thought for the first time that he was sort of funny really. But he sure did smell bad. He'd never be able to take Maizey there to meet his crazy grandfather, even though he was certain that she would think he was funny too. Girls all smell like flowers and such, he thought, and she'd never be able to stand the smell of it there no matter how funny she thought he was.

Aidan was still thinking of Maizey and the armies of angry Catholics when he crossed his own yard and finally arrived at home. Home; he never thought he would see it again and he couldn't wait to tell Doran all about his adventure. He walked inside to find his mother passed out on her bed and Doran stoking the fire.

"Where you been?" Doran asked.

"Where's Pa?" Aidan said as he struggled to get out of his coat. It had become twisted around his arm and he couldn't get out of it. He thought he might have to pull his own arm off.

"We were out working at the dump when the storms come up last night. He sent me home to take care of the wood for Ma. He didn't want to leave the pile of iron we'd collected and lose it in the snowdrift until spring, so he was gonna haul it all to one of grandpa's sheds. He said to tell ma that if the storm got any worse that he would just stay there with Grandpa. So I told her and she got drunk of course. She's been asleep there all morning yet."

Doran shut the door on the fire and turned to his brother, "So where you been?"

"Oh Shit, Doran," Aidan screamed as his eyes grew big as dinner plates and he threw his coat back on. "Damn it! Come on, Doran! We've get to the God damned dump!" He yelled as he grabbed his hat and scarf.

"What is it?" Doran asked while grabbing his own coat and bundle of winter clothes that sat piled by the door.

"It's Pa, Doran! I think something's happened to Pa!" With that they ran out the door and back across the yard, following the fresh trail of footprints down the path that led to the dump.

As the boys approached the door to Collin's shanty, Aidan grabbed his brother to stop him from bolting through the door. "No Doran! He thinks people are coming for him," Aidan said.

"Grandpa," the boys shouted for him first to lessen the chance of getting a shotgun shell in the face and then tried knocking on the door. As they knocked, it swung open and they cautiously went inside. There were no tin can alarms or iron bar propping the door shut and their grandfather was nowhere to be found. "Grandpa," they yelled again into the empty shed. There was no reply. There was only the clanging sound of the tin roof blowing in the wind.

They made their way to the rear of the shed. Aidan began moving garbage and debris that had been stacked against the back door. Then as he unlatched the makeshift door handle, the wind blew it wide open and it slammed against the back wall, shaking the entire structure.

"Grandpa!" they yelled again out the back door, but there was only the sound of the wind whistling through the tin and walls and the loose tin roof clanging.

"What is that, little brother?" Doran asked, pointing around his shoulder to a dark spot in the snow behind the shed.

"God damn it, Doran, No," Aidan dove to the ground and began to clear the snow away. Doran threw himself into the task beside him. They threw their gloves and dug with their bare hands in the cold, hard packed snow.

As they dug around the old, worn leather boots that been sticking out of the snow drift, they slowly uncovered the legs of a man. They both knew who it was by the boots alone, but they dug on and revealed the pants that they knew as well. Then they uncovered the worn, cracked leather jacket that their father had always worn. For most of the year he would wear that jacket, only adding more layers underneath as the winter progressed.

As they dug around his arms, Doran had tried to lift one to see if he could be roused, but it was stiff as a board and solid as a tree limb. Finally they uncovered his head and revealed his wavy brown hair matted with a thick, stiff frozen layer of blood. The side of his head had been crushed and there was a huge dent that was covered in mottled blood and tiny chunks of bone.

Finally, the boys got him uncovered and they rolled his stiff body over. His eyes were wide open, his mouth slightly agape. Aidan thought that he could almost hear him cursing their grandfather while laying there. He envisioned his father's last moment and the split second that he realized that the man that he hated so much would be the end of him in the last place on earth that he wanted to die.

Chapter 18   Blood Red Yellow

The sheriff had come from Albia that night with a deputy and investigated it all. Along with the help of some locals, they would find the old man clutching his shotgun in nothing but his dirt stained long johns, frozen to death, sitting under an old tree by the family burial plot. He had finally got to rest from a lifetime of paranoia and fear, finally gone home to be with his people.

Aidan felt something change in him that day. Something just sort of clicked inside of him and he knew that he would never be the same again. Strange thing was that he wasn't even really sad about losing his father. In some way, Aidan figured that everyone got what they wanted. Grandpa wasn't afraid or crazy anymore. He had always called them by the names of his long dead sons, so Aidan figured that he would be happy to be with them. He even took his other son with him too so he wouldn't have to be so unhappy anymore.

He didn't know much about where you went when you died, and he didn't believe much in churches or God the way they said it was. Somehow though, he knew that they were alright. For him, he felt a sense of freedom that he had never imagined before. He felt a maturity that he had never known. He wouldn't have his father heaping the weight of his own failures upon his shoulders to carry around any longer. There wouldn't be any expectations to prove anything to anyone. He wouldn't have to be one of the Demons of the Dump any more either; only a young man named Aidan.

As for Doran, well, he could just be the nice young man that works at the dump named Doran. After all, people took to Doran sort of natural like, but his association with Papa and Grandpa had always put folks off who might otherwise have got to know him better. Aidan knew that he would never leave the dump though. Doran loved it too much. He felt like a treasure hunter every day. Each night he would tell Aidan all about how much scrap he had found that day, or what new treasures he had discovered.

"Can you believe that someone would just throw something like that away?" He'd say. "Why that's just crazy! I bet I could get a dime out of it right now if I took it Chariton and sold it."

But aside from the scrap, he never took anything anywhere and sold it. Instead, he only piled his private treasures in the room that the boys shared. He piled wide and high until there was but a path hardly wider than a body could walk through to get to bed. Then, just when Aidan thought there wasn't room for anything else, he'd come in late one night and hit his shin on something else that Doran had decided to drag home.

"Can you believe somebody would just throw that away?" He'd say with a proud, gleaming smile.

"No. I can't hardly believe it at all," Aidan would say as he lie in bed holding his bleeding shin close to his body, wondering how badly it was going to be swollen by morning.

Their mother would say later that she was glad the bastard was finally gone. She would drink a lot more and she almost never left the house. She mostly just lay around cursing at the walls and drinking whenever she wasn't passed out asleep. There were other times early in the morning when she'd wake up long before the sun came up too. The boys could hear her crying and moaning and asking why he had left her all alone. She'd keep them awake that way for an hour or even two sometimes, but by the time morning rolled around, she'd be well on her way to drunk again and cursing old Merril.

For his part, Aidan decided that he should try to keep the promises he had made to his father. He would keep going to the school in town and try his damnedest to make him proud. Besides, he still needed an excuse to walk by Maizey's house every afternoon. He still hated that God forsaken school though. He even secretly wished that every single one of the nuns would drop over dead, but something had definitely changed inside of him. He felt...different.

The day after they saw Papa and Grandpa both buried at the old family plot, the boys had talked it over and decided not to lie around the house listening to Ma. "She's gone crazy," Doran said, "and she'll make you crazy too if you sit around here listening to her all of the time."

So, Doran returned to the dump the very next day and Aidan, to school. Still, something was very different about Aidan. He walked to school that morning thinking of Pa and of Maizey, and of Maizey's father. It was bullshit, he had thought. There wasn't anything fair about it that he should have to take shit from his father and the God damned nuns, and the kids at school, only to turn around and have some mule headed ass chase him out of his house because of something some God damned priest had said. God damn kneelers anyways, he thought, the whole lot of them.

He hadn't paid any attention to the time that morning as he walked across the school yard. He hadn't thought about the other boys that day at all, except to curse them under his breath. He'd better watch that, he had thought to himself; curse folks under your breath too much and you'll end up just like Grandpa!

WOOOOOOOOSHT!!

One of Papa's Methodist friends had been in the Great War over there somewhere. He was a funny looking sort because he'd had an Austrian shell blow up right next to his right ear. It took half his face off and there wasn't anything left of the ear, just a wrinkled up hole where it once had been. He used to tell stories about it too; said it felt and sounded like his whole head had been blown off. Then it was followed by a god awful sharp stinging pain and the loudest ringing sound he'd ever heard.

Aidan thought for certain that he would reach up to find that half his head was missing. He must've been hit with a shell like the one that had blown that fellas' face off in the war. He reached up to feel for his ear and felt the stinging and the ringing. He expected to feel blood and bone pieces like they'd seen on Papa's head, but there were only chunks of snow and ice. He cleared it out of his ear as best he could and bent over some, holding his ear. When he looked up and saw the two boys there laughing, he realized that they had struck him with a hard packed ice ball.

He couldn't hear what they were saying over the ringing in his head, but he could see their lips moving as they stood over him pointing and laughing. One of them shoved him just then and everything changed in an instant.

Aidan didn't see visions of Maizey in his head this time. He didn't see her smiling face, or hear her laughter. Instead, he saw his father standing over him with a buggy whip swinging at him. He saw the boys hitting and kicking him and his brother. He saw the Reverend Mother with her evil grimace and her wooden paddle. He saw an image of a priest standing in front of a thousand Catholics warning them of some little boy in a God damned yellow shirt that he had never even laid eyes on.

As the boys moved in and one shoved him, Aidan closed his eyes and tried to think of Maizey, but the other pictures remained in his head. He felt the blow to his head of a fist and he felt the rage deep inside of him as it boiled over. When he opened his eyes again, one of the boys lay on the ground bleeding with a broken nose. The other one struggled to crawl away, crying. Aidan hit the one with the broken nose one more time square in the face for good measure. Then standing, he walked toward the other boy. The boy held his stocking cap in his gloved hand. Turning, he looked at Aidan through an eye that was already beginning to swell shut. Aidan could see him mouthing something, but he could still hear only the high pitched screaming ringing sound. He kicked the boy in his ribs then reared back and kicked him once in the face, rolling him onto his back where he laid holding his mouth and sobbing.

Everything was different now. That day during the lunch hour, the Reverend Mother waited as she had a dozen times before for all the boys to assemble. She gave a speech about evil and a lot of other shit. Then she had Aidan lean forward while she struck him with the paddle. He did not cry out, hell, he didn't cry at all. He didn't even let out a sound. Instead, with each blow he glared even deeper into the eyes of the boys in the lunchroom. One by one, he stared them down until all eyes were on the floor.

He was Aidan Keane, by God. Of the junk yard Keanes, sure enough and they couldn't hurt him any more.

That evening when he got home he found his mother passed out on the floor of the kitchen again. He stepped over her and stoked the fire to warm the house for Doran. Doran had decided to get home early that night to see his brother and walked in right behind him as Aidan was still taking off his coat.

"Oh my God Aidan," he said, "What the hell happened to you today?"

"What do you mean?" Aidan asked.

"Your shirt, it's covered. The God damned thing is blood red yellow!" He said. "Are you alright? What happened to ya?"

"Oh, that," Aidan replied looking down at his shirt, "Yeah, I'm fine. It's not my blood."

Chapter 19   Drive

By the end of the following month, as a result of the urgent appeal of concerned parents throughout Melrose, Aidan was expelled from school. The Reverend Mother, finally beaten by Aidan's ability to withstand the cruelest of punishments without so much as a flinch, was more than happy to be rid of the boy. His tolerance of pain and gritty new self determination proved too much for the nuns to control any longer. In short, their reign of sadistic fun torturing the heathen boy to sell their style of fear of God to the other boys was finally over.

When he walked out of the school that final day, even the boys three or four years his elder would not stop to taunt him any longer. It was too much of a risk, they figured, to pick on a boy who was guaranteed to fight you like a wildcat. Because no matter how big or how much older you were, there was always at least a chance that he would win somehow, and how would that look? No. It was best, especially if you were much older and bigger than him, to simply leave him be. As Aidan exited the building he tore the yellow shirt from his body and threw it on the schoolhouse walk. He'd never enter that building, or wear *anything* yellow again.

Everyone knew what had happened to the Gowery boy too. He'd come to find Aidan after he'd beaten his brother and his friend. Jimmy Gowery was 15 at the time and Aidan was only eleven. But Aidan had beaten Jimmy's little brother, the 13 year old Brendan Gowery and his friend, 13 year old Patrick O'Neal over some incident involving a snow ball of all things. So Jimmy, to defend the family honor it would seem, waited for Aidan on the road that he traveled out of town each day. They say that Aidan fancied some girl on up the road, but no one knew for sure why he walked so far out of the way. Whatever the reason, Jimmy Gowery didn't care much.

As Aidan passed that night near the edge of town, Jimmy stepped out into the road behind him and yelled at the younger boy to stop. Aidan turned around just as Jimmy was upon him. As Jimmy drew back to swing, his arm suddenly locked behind him. It would seem that Jimmy was not the only one waiting for Aidan that day on the lonely stretch of dirt road. For Doran had stepped out as well, just in time to see Jimmy approaching his younger brother to ambush him.

They say that Jimmy Gowery had to crawl home that night he was beaten so badly. Both he and his brother would receive good beatings from their own father as well for having made him the laughing stock of Melrose. Two sons aged 13 and 15, both beaten by the same small 11 year old dump boy. The Gowery name was tarnished near beyond repair.

After Aidan had been expelled from school, he continued to leave the house each morning as though he was still enrolled. At night, he would return at the same time as he had before too. Each way he would walk the long road by Maizey May Mullan's house. As the winter gave way to ever warmer days, Aidan kept expecting to eventually see her outside. He always looked for her to be hiding in the ditch, or up near the house, but he never saw her. Once, he had seen her mother outside though. The woman had only turned her back the minute she saw him, yelling something toward the house.

During the days, he'd go and toss about Melrose. There wasn't much to do there most days for a young man without a penny to his name. Sometimes he would get to watch grown men beating hell out of one another outside of one the taverns. On warmer days, he could watch a game of dice being thrown in one of the alleyways behind the main thoroughfare. Some days he'd just walk the railroad tracks for miles on end.

He liked to look down the long, straight stretches of track that seemed to go on as far as the earth itself over the horizon. He used to wonder where they went to and if the whole rest of the world was like Melrose. Often times, as the trains passed by, he'd step off the track just enough to let it pass and feel the wind blow in his face from the cars as they sped by. One day, he might just damned well grab hold of a slow one, he'd think to himself. He could feel himself blow right with that wind to some far away place. Then the train, and the wind would be gone, and Aidan would still be standing there.

It was on a fine sunny spring day that Aidan had been out walking the tracks, when he turned down the road that led by Maizey's house to do his daily afternoon walk by. He thought of her smile again and her golden locks and her shining eyes. How he loved those eyes. On up the road, where a spring kept it bogged with thick mud year round, there was a truck with its' hind end stuck hub deep. An old man stood nearby rubbing his face with his hat and scratching his head.

Aidan walked up behind him and spoke so not to startle the old goat.

"Hello, sir," Aidan called out, "something I can do to help?"

"Yes! Young man! As a matter of fact! Would you happen to know how to drive because if you can put her into gear, I can use this here beam to lever her on out." The old man was full of piss and vinegar and he smiled as he spoke as a man who hadn't a care in the world. If Aidan hadn't seen the thing, he'd have never known that this jovial old coot was stuck in the mud at all.

"No sir," Aidan said smiling, "I never even been in a car or truck before, let alone made one go."

"Well son, this here is your lucky day then I reckon," he said, "Because if'n you want, I'd like to teach you how. Ross MacGregor is the name," he said, reaching out to shake hands. The part of the old man's forearm that stuck out of his shirt as he reached was long and lean and terrible mean looking. It looked like nothing but sinew and tendons covered in stretched, thin aging rawhide.

"The name is Aidan, sir," he replied, "Aidan Keane, Pleasure to meet you."

"The pleasure is all mine, laddy," Ross replied.

There was something odd in the way he had said laddy though. Aidan had heard the talk of a lot of men from the old country. He'd never heard anyone talk like this before though.

"What is it laddy? You look perplexed boy!" He smiled still through his thick, dark red moustache.

"If it aint too rude of me to ask, what part of Ireland are you from Mr. MacGregor?" He inquired.

"Ahhh," he bellowed in laughter, "Ireland?!?!?! You've never heard an Irishman around these parts who sounds like me have you boy?"

"No sir, I haven't," Aidan replied.

"I'm from Scotland lad! And if'n you were older and bigger I'd have to challenge you to a duel for offending my honor boy!" He laughed. "Why, those are fighting words you know! Be damned if I'll be compared to a bunch of God damned kneelers!"

Aidan laughed at the antics of the old man. He was the most animated character he'd ever seen. MacGregor's moustache was so long and thick that you could only see his bottom lip. When he raised his voice the center part of the moustache would fly up in front of his nose from the wind of his breath. Best of all, his huge, dinner plate blue eyes would get big and round as turnips as he spoke.

"My people used to call em' kneelers too," Aidan said chuckling a little.

"Ah," MacGregor replied, "then you must be from sound stock boy."

"I never heard of no place called Scotland before, sir." Aidan said.

"What?" The old man replied, feigning anger. "Tis of no wonder, I reckon, being schooled in these parts amongst so many of the bastards. We Scots are a free people you see lad. We are proud and free, whereas these kneelers of the Irish bent, well...," His eyes grew wide as he spoke and then squinted them almost closed as he leaned in toward Aidan. "If you'll kneel before a man a half a world away in a pointy hat, then you'll kneel before the English monarchy, and anyone who will do that, well, I reckon they'll pert near kneel before anybody, won't they boy?" With that MacGregor's eyes grew wide again and he bellowed with laughter.

Aidan only smiled and shook his head. He wasn't sure what to make of this fellow with his funny sounding words, but he knew that he liked him a great deal. Aidan could always tell right away if he was going to like someone or not. It was sort of a gift that he had. Thing was; Aidan very rarely met anyone that he liked, and never took to anyone like this MacGregor fellow right off before.

"Alright then lad, we'd best get this here truck a moving again! You jump on up in the front seat there," MacGregor opened the door of the old truck. It was huge inside and reeked of pipe tobacco.

Aidan felt his stomach begin to knot up with nervous excitement as he sat behind the wheel looking out the windshield at the road laid out ahead of him. Everything about the truck seemed enormous to him. That any single man, or even a boy, could get into a cab and control something so large with just a few pedals and levers seemed unthinkable to him. He'd never thought of it before, but now that he was sitting there behind the wheel, Aidan was awestruck at the sheer size of the machine and power of the operator.

MacGregor shut the door and stood on the running board beside him, spitting in Aidan's ear and flopping his moustache as he explained what the different pedals and levers did and how to operate the thing.

"Alright lad, now let's you give it a try just like I showed you." MacGregor said enthusiastically.

Aidan's hands shook as he depressed the clutch and turned the key in the ignition. The giant green monster sputtered and screamed and rumbled to life. Aidan was taken aback at how the thing vibrated his entire body and he looked to MacGregor to see if everything was working right, or if the thing was fixing to explode and kill them both. MacGregor, for his part, seemed unaffected by the sounds, so Aidan figured that it must all be normal.

"Alright lad, now do like I told you," MacGregor yelled over the sputtering engine. He was still hanging on the driver's side so his lips were only a few inches from Aidan's ear, but he kept on yelling nonetheless. "You just let off the clutch and give some gas now boy!"

Aidan looked down at the different pedals trying to remember which was which. He couldn't imagine how anyone could actually drive one of these things, keep track of so many levers and pedals, AND steer the thing. It seemed like a two man job if ever he'd seen one. As his foot slowly let off the clutch, the other pushed down on the gas. Nothing happened. Aidan turned to look at MacGregor to see if he had done something wrong and the clutch engaged. The truck lurched forward violently and died. MacGregor was gone.

"MacGregor?" Aidan yelled, as the old man flew off the side of truck and into the dirt road below Aidan's view.

MacGregor's head re-emerged a few seconds later showing a huge embarrassed smile under his moustache. "Good try lad! Now let's do it all again whilst I pry on the back of the thing."

"I don't know, sir, I..." Aidan said.

"Nonsense, boy! You're doing a magnificent job. Just do the same thing over and again until you get it right. You'll get it. And for God sake boy, don't go calling me sir no more. I feel old enough as it is. Call me MacGregor if you like, or anything else you prefer, anything but sir. There are no sirs, nor madams in this country. We're all equal. Free AND equal. Each mother's son of us! Now I'm going to pry on her," MacGregor disappeared behind the truck and continued to talk, but Aidan couldn't tell what he was saying.

"All right, give her hell boy," the old man yelled from behind the truck.

Aidan repeated the steps as he'd done before and the truck lurched forward again and died. On his next attempt the truck rolled forward a good foot before he killed it. He had hoped that it would be good enough so MacGregor could get it out the rest of the way himself. Aidan leaned out the window and looked behind him. MacGregor was leaned around the back of the truck looking at him expectantly.

"Excellent lad! One more time and we'll have it I think!" He smiled again, trying to reassure his reluctant helper before he leapt out of the cab and disappeared down the road. "Just try it once more boy. I'll get another bite on it here under the left tire this time."

"Okay," Aidan yelled back shaking his head and near sick to his stomach with nervousness. Looking down at the gear shifter he tried to remember which way MacGregor had showed him to move the thing. It should be easy enough to remember, he had just done it three times. The sweat began to form on his forehead. He was losing his mind, he thought. He looked down at the gas and clutch and brake and couldn't, for the life of him, remember which was which. Panic set in as he heard MacGregor hollering from behind him to, "Go-Go-Go!"

"God damn it all to hell," Aidan said as he pushed down on the clutch and started the old truck up again. He reached for the shifter and felt it slip into gear. Then, slowly he let off the clutch as he pushed down on the gas. He heard MacGregor yelling something inaudible as he felt the wheels begin to engage. Aidan found him in his side mirror just in time to see him leap out of the way as the truck barreled out of the mud and back onto the road...in reverse.

It took Aidan a second to realize that he was in reverse, another to realize that he was still going, and a third to remember that HE was driving. By the time the fourth second rolled around, he'd drove backwards into the opposite side ditch and had stalled the old truck out by pressing his feet on all the pedals he could until *something* happened.

Aidan was certain that he'd run over MacGregor and the old man was lying atop the road dead. The ditch was an easy embankment with no trees or mud, but just deep enough that he couldn't see over the crest of the road. Aidan leaped from the truck and ran out of the ditch on to the road. There, he discovered MacGregor lying along the side of the road covered in mud and laughing so hard that he couldn't breathe. At first, Aidan had thought him to be blood red and crying in pain, but upon closer inspection, he found the old coot to only be beat red due to lack of breath from laughing at him.

"I thought you were hurt," Aidan said, pretending to be frowning.

"Oh, my land boy, if you could've seen your face as you drove into that ditch! I've been around this world and THAT, young Keane, was the damnedest thing I ever seen," MacGregor said, still laughing so hard that tears run down his cheeks and spit covered the ends of his moustache. "Now, that, my boy deserves a dinner! Help me up out of this here mud lad, and we'll go and celebrate!"

Aidan reached down, himself red with embarrassment, and helped MacGregor to his feet. "I told you I never drove before," he said.

"Well, you have now, haven't you boy?!?!" The old man replied, still smiling and wiping tears away.

"Yes sir, I reckon I have at that," Aidan replied with a bit of a smile of his own.

"If you have the time then lad, let's go and grab a bite to eat. I'm half starved!" MacGregor replied. "Oh, and I'll do the driving this time!"

They laughed together as they walked back down the ditch and climbed into the truck. Yes. Aidan definitely took to him. He'd nearly killed him twice already, but he liked him nonetheless.

The old truck fired up and pulled easily out of the ditch. As it turned back onto the road and geared up to speed, Aidan looked at the road and wondered what else lay ahead for him, in the road and in his life. *Was* there a world outside of Melrose? Were there more people like

MacGregor out there who didn't care that he was Aidan Keane, of the dump devil Keanes? One day, by God, he'd find out. Melrose was already getting too small for him. He'd already be gone too, if it weren't for Doran...and Maizey.

Chapter 20   Devil No More

As the old truck barreled along, Aidan spotted a figure ahead of them in the road. Growing nearer, he squinted as the form came into view. It was a familiar form, walking away from them but...

"Stop the truck!" Aidan yelled.

"What? But laddy, we've only a bit further to..."

"Stop the damned truck MacGregor!" he screamed desperately.

With that the truck screeched to a halt and a cloud of dust ascended high into the air, then settled down around the figure and Aidan himself as he leaped out onto the road.

"Maizey!" He hollered into the cloud of dust around them.

"Aidan? Is that you?" She replied.

With that the dust settled and they came into full view of one another. Maizey stood before him in the green dress and pullover of the Melrose Catholic School for Girls. Her beautiful curly hair had turned to a shade of dark auburn over the winter, with little trace of the shining blonde that took over in the summer months. The green of her shirt and the shade of her hair made her beautiful green eyes shine like emeralds in the late morning sun.

Aidan had waited for this moment for what seemed like an eternity and here she was, finally standing before him alone in the road.

"Ah, she's quite a beauty, that one is, lad!" MacGregor called out the passenger side window.

Aidan turned and glared at his friend until his gaze had singed the hair on his overgrown moustache. MacGregor slowly sat back in his seat and looked in the opposite direction. Aidan was mortified and he could feel his face change color as every drop of blood in his body rushed to his head.

"Funny," Maizey said with that huge smile of hers, "you don't look like no devil I ever heard of before. Papa said you was a devil, but I know better than that. You're no devil at all. I think you're..."

"Uh, lad you'd better..." MacGregor yelled out the window again.

"Damn it, MacGregor, will you give me a minute, for God's sake. I..." Aidan turned to glare at his friend once more only to find him leaned well over in the cab again, this time pointing out across the vast expanse of field behind him. Aidan followed the path of MacGregor's finger as it directed his eyes over Aidan's own shoulder and... "Oh shit!" He yelled.

Aidan turned to see Maizey's father steadily jogging toward the road yelling something that couldn't be understood over the sound of the truck's idling engine. Her father was waving something over his head as he trotted closer, but Aidan figured he needn't stick around to see what exactly it was. He leaped back onto the truck's side board and opened the door.

"Get us out of here, MacGregor! Go! Go! Go!" He screamed as the truck slipped into gear. Still hanging off the side of the moving truck Aidan turned back toward Maizey just as her father was within yards of the road wielding a hoe. "I ain't no devil Maizey," He yelled at her.

"I know," she yelled back as the truck shifted into second and began to tear away.

"Maizey! I love you!" Aidan yelled, and with that he threw himself into the truck and slammed the door, watching in the rearview mirror as her father led her by the arm, walking on toward their house.

Even Aidan knew that he was too young to really love someone the way that older folks do. Still, nothing or no one had ever touched his heart the way that Maizey had before. He wished he'd had time to explain what he had meant and how he felt about her. It's hard to say what love *is*. It was even harder for Aidan to imagine that there was any emotion more powerful than what he felt for her then. As much as a boy his age could, or knew how, or was aware of though, he loved her, wholly and completely.

No sooner had the truck gotten up to speed, than it began to slow down again. Aidan looked out across the rolling expanses of winter wheat field just coming on for the spring, followed by a vast pasture with hundreds of sheep, some of whom had just given birth.

"Why are we slowing down?" He turned to MacGregor, his own heart still pounding from the excitement.

"Because, laddy," he smiled, "We're home!" And with that he swung wide into the driveway.

"Oh my god, you're neighbors with...!" Aidan said, frightened that he might have jumped out of the frying pan only to have landed into the fire.

"Relax lad," MacGregor smiled reassuringly, "that damned kneeler knows well enough to not show his face on this property. You're safe from his ilk here boy. His face still aches from the close shave he got last fall when he came around here to moan about this and that! No, he'll not be coming over here to get ya; that much I can promise you, lad." MacGregor roared with laughter at his own private joke.

"What do you mean by a close shave?" Aidan asked.

"Aye," MacGregor replied smiling as he reached under his loose fitting pants by his ankle and produced a large knife from a sheath. He drew it up to his own face and flicked the edge of the blade along the whiskers on his cheek. "A close shave," he said laughing again. "Held him firm against that tree there yonder and took off an inch or two of his whiskers, I did! I told the pious kneeling bastard that if he comes back around lookin' for trouble here, the shaves were only goin' to get closer too!" He added, bursting into a giggle as he sheathed his knife.

"Oh," Aidan replied.

"He's a harmless blowhard boy and a God damned kneeler to boot, but he sure does have him one beautiful daughter, eh ?" He smiled once more before shutting off the truck and climbing out.

For the first time Aidan realized that the old man was missing half the teeth in his head behind that overgrown moustache of his. It explained why he spat so much when he hollered at him through the window.

"Yes. She is. Her name is Maizey," Aidan said, thoughtfully re-membering every detail of her as she stood on the road. "I love her," he added, feeling a new confidence after having blurted it out alongside the road.

"So I've heard lad," MacGregor said, climbing down the side of truck to the ground.

Aidan opened his door and climbed out his side, meeting MacGregor in front of the truck.

"I just wouldn't expect to collect much of a dowry from her Pa by the looks of things!" The old man laughed again, bellowing this time, in full amusement at himself.

Aidan laughed at the thought of Maizey's father having to pay him a dowry as was the custom amongst the Irish. "No, I reckon not," he retorted happily. "I reckon not."

Aidan had wished that he had more time to tell Maizey how he felt about her. He wanted to tell her how often he thought of her, how she had become his guardian angel through so many troubled times. He wanted to tell her how he dreamed of each curly lock of her hair, and those beautiful shining eyes of hers. He wished he could have told her that the memory of her smile alone shined brightly into the darkest corners of his existence and warmed his very soul. He had wanted to say so many things, but he'd only blurted out that he loved her. Perhaps that was enough, he thought to himself.

"But I aint no devil to her," he said aloud to himself. "And if I ain't no devil to her, then I ain't a devil no more at all, no matter what any other body thinks. To hell with them."

"Aye lad," MacGregor smiled a faint smile. Leaning in as he squinted a good look into Aidan's eyes, he added, "I've known a devil or two in my day too boy. But you haven't a drop of one in ya. If there ever was any, there ain't a devil no more. I'd know it if there was too!" He finished, shaking his finger in Aidan's face as he spoke.

Chapter 21   Quail & Mutton Hog

As the spring and summer of 1927 progressed, Aidan found himself spending more and more of his days helping MacGregor around his sprawling farm. There was little else productive to do anyhow, and it got him out of the house away from his mother and her worsening alcoholism.

Doran had kept on at the dump and begged Aidan to come and work with him scrapping and salvaging, but Aidan felt obliged to remain true to his word to his father and steer clear of it. While he never worked there per say, by mid-summer, he and Doran had taken up living in one of grandpa's old lean-tos full time. They had fixed it up to meet their needs and burnt enough candles and wood inside to finally smoke out the old person smell and make it tolerable to human senses once more.

For food, the boys ate the meat that MacGregor had used as payment for most of the work that Aidan did. It was sheep meat, or mutton as it was called, but it tasted horrible gamey, so it only served as backup for the days when they couldn't catch a fish out of old man McDougal's pond or shoot something more table worthy.

It was during these days that Aidan developed his lifelong affection for hunting and trapping. Furs were good money then, no matter how scarce, so at night the boys ran trap line for coons and fox and beaver and whatever else was about. With the roaring twenties in full bloom and every dapper gentleman in the cities requiring a fur coat more extravagant than the last, hundreds of Southern Iowans supplemented their incomes with trapping for furs. It meant a lot of competition for scarcer and scarcer game, but it also meant that a load of fifty large, high grade raccoons to the St. Louis market could fetch enough to buy you a new Model A Ford. But then again, fifty coon pelts were damned hard to come by.

With a single shot shotgun they had inherited from their father, and another double barrel that had been pried from the hands of their dead grandfather, the boys hunted the roads and back lots almost every evening. The deer were almost non-existent in Southern Iowa then. For the lucky few who had ever laid eyes on one in those years, it could serve as fodder for a hundred bar room stories. What was in abundance, and made for fine eating was squirrel and bobwhite quail.

It seemed then that every draw of brush held fifty to a hundred quail in it. Two boys need merely walk down any draw to the end to 'flush' them out and force the covey of quail to 'break' into flight. Some of their fondest times and memories spent together were spent fishing, trapping, and hunting the majestic slow rolling wooded hills all around them.

Aidan did not see much of Maizey that year, or the next. Her father and mother knew that he was spending regular time with MacGregor right down the lane so they had kept her under even tighter wraps than normal. MacGregor, for his part, did what he could to calm the situation by hurling curses and colorful epitaphs over the fence to Maizey's father whenever he saw him close enough to hear.

By summer's end MacGregor asked Aidan to come and work for him full-time on his growing spread. MacGregor was due to expand his operation, he'd said, and he was hell bent on buying a new tractor in the spring to do it with too. Aidan readily accepted the position to be paid equally in cash and mutton (which Aidan and Doran had already learned to hate). They had figured however, that they could fatten out a good hog by feeding the thing a mash of grain and dried mutton, so not all was a total loss on the deal.

As the winter of 1927-28 set in upon the hills of Southern Iowa, Aidan, who'd just turned 12 years old, had finally learned to start and drive the old truck...in the forward gears.

Chapter 22   Panic

In the spring of 1928, be damned if old MacGregor didn't go out and buy himself a brand new McCormick-Deering tractor right out of the catalog. It was the fanciest thing that nearly any of the local farmers had ever seen before. In droves they'd drive or ride by, sometimes several times a day just to watch him work with it. He scared hell out of Aidan with it though, because old MacGregor insisted on always riding standing upright, turned round to watch the gear pull behind him.

More and more, MacGregor became Aidan's surrogate father. More and more, Aidan would split his evenings between the dump with Doran and the MacGregor spread. MacGregor too, was a hunter. Thing was though, is he insisted on hunting in full Scottish attire, which included kilt and hat. Both made of the finest (but most God awful colorful) wool that Aidan had ever seen.

In October of 1929, the stock market crashed and it was all the rave of folks to talk about. They say that's when the Great Depression had begun, but with the exception of falling fur prices, neither Doran, nor Aidan, seemed to notice much. Many of the folks in the hills of Southern Iowa were already dirt poor. They had already been living hand to mouth prior to the beginning of the so called "Great Depression."

As Aidan would succinctly put it years later, "We couldn't see what was so great about it at all."

In later years he had little sympathy for the 'good old days.' When decades had passed and a man said to him one day, "I remember when a loaf of bread cost a dime and today you can't buy one for two dollars!" Aidan had replied, "Yeah, well I've got two dollars right here in my pocket, but who in the hell ever had a dime back then?!?!"

The boys and men who earned their keep in the Southern Iowa hills had but two different times to recall of the era, lean times, and even leaner ones. There were times when you had little to eat and times when you had nothing at all. There were times when a single quail had served as the daily meal for both boys, and times when they wished they had a quail to split. But there were also times when their plates were full of fresh mutton and they wished they had anything else!

In 1931 and on into 1933, the bank runs began. People would just get antsy and all of a sudden all go to the bank one morning. Then folks would start talking about a line at the bank and would they have enough money? Before you knew it, they really didn't. They called them 'runs' and 'panics' and they spread like wildfires all across the country.

Fortunately, MacGregor had never believed in banks to begin with, so his money was safe, but as they kept printing more of it, even his stockpile of greenbacks shrank in value with each new moon. MacGregor talked often of gold and silver as well, but even that could not save you then from the wolves as the government began messing with gold standards and daily rates.

It was that summer though, the summer of 1933 that would be marked by Aidan decades later as one of the best and worst years of his life all rolled into one. Of all of the years, all of the decades, none would change and define his life more than 1933. It would not be his defining year alone though, for once again in his young life, everything was about to change...

Chapter 23   1933

That time in Aidan's life had carried on as an autumn leaf floating gently down a slow flowing stream. The years between 1927 and 1933 were the best of his young life. They were filled with MacGregor's laughter and warm smile, and his best friend and brother, Doran. He and Doran had grown up in a time and a place that was ripe for the plucking. Adventurous young men could hunt and fish and trap without interference or oversight from a plethora of parents, landowners, and laws.

There were a hundred funny stories from the farm, like the time MacGregor had tried to leap the fence and grab a sheep that had gotten out. His boot had caught on the top wire though, right as he got a hand on the animal. The antics that resulted looked as if someone had tried to build a failed crossbow designed specifically to launch old Scots.

Likewise, Aidan and Doran had shared a thousand adventures; like the time they were cleaning the outbuildings at the dump and discovered Grandpa's hidden still and a lifetime supply of rotgut. Doran must have puked for three days the first time they had dared to drink it. He had thought he would die for sure. Aidan, on the other hand, had only fell down and passed out. He had woken fine as frog hair the following morning and had great fun the next 48 hours trying to make Doran throw up again.

As for Maizey, he had been content to see her whenever she could steal away a moment to exchange glances and smiles on the road or in town. Always, she remained under the constant and vigilant eyes of her parents though. He was content however, in knowing, that she was never further than across the fence from the MacGregor spread.

As the depression had deepened, MacGregor became increasingly short on cash to pay for Aidan's labor. The mutton remained painfully plentiful however and MacGregor assured him that he was keeping close account of his earnings and how much was owed. Aidan was fine with the arrangement as he had room and board as much as he required of it and nowhere else to go anyhow. Besides, he had grown to love the old man like the father that he'd never had.

In fact, it had been while he was out fixing MacGregor's fence along the road when everything changed. What began on that day in Aidan's 16th year would change his life forever.

It was the second week in April of 1933. It was easy to remember because the morel mushrooms had come early that year. The small grey morels that rose first out of the ground each spring had arrived in full force only the week before. MacGregor had taken to the local fare in the form of mushrooms years before. As a result, MacGregor had saved the bulk of the fence checking assignment for Aidan for when the mushrooms were coming up. That way the boy could serve the dual purpose of repairing fence and picking mushrooms as he went.

Aidan had finally finished repairing the holes in the last fence line along the northern border of MacGregor's farm. As he turned to follow the fence back south along the road, he saw them. It was incredible. Never before had he seen anything like it. He would talk about the discovery for the rest of his life, in fact.

Sprawled out before him were hundreds of small yellow mushrooms along the ditch for as far as his eyes could focus to see them. It was along a stretch they had only just cleared of trees and brush the year before. With the cover removed from the soft, moist earth, and almost nowhere to hide, hundreds of morels shone brightly before him in the early afternoon sun.

111

They grew to the north and to the south. They were along the fence row and in the field. They grew down the ditch embankment and back up the other side along the road. As he looked at what all lay before him, he even saw some growing in the road itself. They were everywhere!

Aidan examined the small clothe sack he had carried with him containing a dozen or so morels. Then he raised the other hand holding the large burlap bag containing a variety of tools and wire for fixing the fence. Without a thought, he dumped the bag of tools and wire onto the ground beside the corner post. Immediately, he was on his knees picking mushrooms.

Slowly and methodically, Aidan crawled down into the ditch clearing a swath of mushrooms. He figured he'd go along the ditch first and pick all the ones that could be viewed from the road. Later, he'd come back with MacGregor and get the ones in the field that others wouldn't be able to see.

As he crawled along, the old burlap sack began to form a slowly growing round lump in the bottom. He must have been picking for half an hour before he made his way to the edge of the road. Crawling through the grass, he reached into the road to pinch one from its base. As he did, he noticed the mud covered boots about a foot further out into the road.

His mind was awash in dreams of mushroom covered fields and bountiful, tasty riches. He had to follow the boots up the legs some before his brain could grasp that they were indeed attached to a person. When he did, he startled and threw himself backwards away from the roadbed. Landing squarely on his rear, he looked up foolishly at the figure that stood before him.

It was her. It was Maizey. She was alone and unguarded and smiling as big and bright a smile as he had ever seen. Her hair was already beginning its annual migration from auburn to light strawberry blonde. Caught somewhere in the midst of its metamorphosis it shone brightly in the afternoon sun. Streaks of golden blonde and strawberry curls bounced atop her head as she laughed.

"Oh my," she said through embarrassed laughter. "I didn't realize that I had grown so frightening since the last time you laid eyes on me."

She was beautiful. She had always been beautiful, but now, well. Now, she was something else. Rising out of the mud boots her smooth pink legs revealed long, slender, muscular, defined calves. The yellow summer dress she wore that day blew against her form in the light wind and revealed the lines of her thighs, the curvature of her hips, and the smallness of her waist. The yellow fabric draped over her breasts and revealed the figure of something more than a girl. Sometime during the long winter, Maizey had become a young woman.

"You aren't frightening at all Maizey," Aidan said, shaking his head imperceptibly to wake himself from his hypnotic daze. "You're. You're the most beautiful thing that I have ever seen."

"I never can believe the things that come out of your mouth Aidan," Maizey replied, feeling her blushing cheeks begin to pulse.

"Where's your...?" He began to ask, but thought best not to.

"My what? My father?" She replied softly.

Aidan shook his head in affirmation as he pulled himself to his feet.

"He has gone back to Ohio to visit with some of our people there. And Mama has her hands full with my baby brother," she said as she cocked her head, suspiciously eyeing Aidan's burlap bag. "Are those all? Why, they can't be," she said in amazement.

"They sure are," he replied. "Look here," he said, walking toward her, opening his sack wide at the top for her to look inside. By then the sack was nearly a third full of small mushrooms.

"Why, there must be a million of them in there!" Maizey gasped.

"I don't know. I've been picking them forever already and haven't even got started yet!" he said. "Look Maizey, just look at them all!" he said, pointing all up and down the edge of the road.

"My goodness," she said looking in amazement wherever Aidan pointed, "I never."

"Me neither, but they're that way all the way back up to the fence and across it even into the field!" Aidan said excitedly after seeing her shared enthusiasm for his legendary discovery. "You want to help me pick em'?"

"Of course," She said enthusiastically, smiling brightly. As she squatted and began to pick the few within her grasp along the road, she looked up at Aidan. He stood staring at the new curves of her body as she stooped. "Daddy won't let me pick them any more you know. He said it wasn't lady-like at my age a few years back."

"That's just plain stupid," Aidan replied. "I think if you like doing it then you had ought to keep right on doing it."

"Me too," She said, smiling at him and looking at him thoughtfully as she plucked another mushroom.

Before long, they were crawling side by side in the ditch and up the hillside to the fence. Her dress soon bore the same grey-brown of the clay in the grader ditch, same as Aidan's clothes and much of his face. She would cup the little treasures in her small gentle hand until it was overflowing, then reach over in front of Aidan. He'd open the sack for her and lean over so she could drop them inside.

"I didn't know you had a baby brother," he said.

"That's because he's new, silly," she replied giggling, "that's why he's my BABY brother."

"Oh yeah, right," Aidan said, making a scrunched, funny face in humorous recognition of his own foolish question.

"Aren't they a little old, your parents I mean?" He asked.

"Yes, they are. They'd thought so too. Even before that time though, they just thought that something had happened so she couldn't have any more young ones after I was born. It happens, like it did with the Riley woman in town. She had that cute little girl that goes by Alice and then she never had another one after that. And Alice is ten or eleven now," Maizey said. When she looked up at Aidan she found his eyes wide and he seemed to be staring right through her. "What is it?" She asked. "What's wrong?"

"Nothing," Aidan replied seriously and thoughtfully, "there aint anything wrong. I've just been dreaming of you forever since we were kids. There is so much that I have wanted to tell you about, so many things that I've wanted to share with you. I've dreamed about finally having the chance to talk to you. I bet I've imagined this very moment in a thousand different places and ways."

"And?" She asked.

"Well, I always just imagined you being quieter," he said, laughing through his huge smile.

"Aidan!" She said, feigning offense. She reached over and gave him a shove.

Aidan had been perched on one knee as he spoke, and her shove, however slight, knocked him off balance. Try as he might to stay upright, he fell over. In an effort to keep from toppling onto the sack or having it fall open, he wound up face first in the moist dirt. Righting himself, there were blades of new growth, bright green grass in his teeth and mud on his nose and cheek.

Maizey roared with laughter at the sight and he was soon to join her. The two sat on the hill for the next several minutes just enjoying their long awaited time together and laughing. It was a beautiful moment for each of them, surrounded by the bright greens of new plants springing to life and the trees all thick with buds.

"I had better get back," she said. "Mama will be wondering where I'm at." She stood and began rubbing dirt and grass off her dress.

"Maizey?" He asked, revealing a hint of desperation in his voice, but cautious of ruining the moment with too much seriousness.

"Yes?" She asked.

Aidan stood up and gazed deeply into her eyes. They were green and heavenly beautiful. For the first time ever, as she stood there only a few feet away looking up at him, he noticed something else. It was something amazing and beautiful, and perfect and wonderful all rolled into one. In the tops of each, spilled in amongst the hues of green were tiny drops of milk chocolate right above the darks of her eyes. They were magnificent and it was as if the left eye had twice as much spilled in it as the right.

Those eyes of hers were as shimmering green emeralds, each with a tiny drop of milk chocolate in them.

Looking into those eyes, Aidan could feel his heart flutter in his chest. Literally, she had taken his breath away and he struggled slightly to regain his composure.

"Do you want to take some of these mushrooms with you, Maizey?" He asked.

"No. You keep them," she replied. "I really have to go, Aidan. Thank you for this. Really," she said as she turned to start back down the road.

"Maizey?" He called after her, not even trying to hide his desperation.

"Yes?" She replied.

"When will I see you again?" He asked.

"Tomorrow," she said, smiling brightly. "I shall walk up this very road tomorrow at noon. I will expect you to tell me all those things you were wanting to tell me, and cook me some of those mushrooms for lunch too!" And with that she turned away, dress twirling, creating an upside down yellow flower, blooming over the roadbed, before it flowed gently down to settle upon her blossoming figure.

"Alright then, I'll be here," he hollered after her.

Aidan stood in awe and watched his own personal angel walk away from him along the road. At one point, too far away even to yell back and forth, she turned back and looked at him still standing there, staring at her. He couldn't see it, but she was smiling brightly and blushed privately to discover him still watching her. She had hoped that he would still be watching her of course. Sure enough, there he was, just as she knew that he would be.

Once she had left the road and disappeared behind the trees to cross the broad lawn leading to her own home, Aidan just stood there for a while. Lighting a cigarette and smiling, he was living his dream. "Tiny drops of milk chocolate," he said to himself as he smoked, "the one on the left twice as much as the one on the right." He blew his smoke and watched it as it drifted slowly away into the rising gentle wind.

Chapter 24   Haggis

Aidan had run all the way back to MacGregor's house that afternoon. He found the old man relaxing and enjoying a drink behind
the house at the long patio table. MacGregor had carved the thing
himself out of a single piece of oak. It sat, where it had fallen years
before, and had been carefully carved and hewn into the form of a
table. The rest of what must have been a grand tree had been cut and
split and thrown into the fire for fuel. Around it, he had laid stones
of every color to form a patio. There he enjoyed to sit in the
evenings under a maple that had grown rapidly in place of the giant
oak, drinking and regaling the boys with stories of his homeland and
long dead Scottish heroes.

Aidan ran up to him, and throwing his tools on the ground near his
feet, dumped the contents of his sack onto the table. "And there are
a million more where these came from," he said smiling.

"Good Lord, boy! You've struck gold, I tell you," he replied in
amazement, rising from his chair and leaning over the table to
inspect the treasure horde.

Aidan always loved it when MacGregor said the word 'you' because
it came out long and drawn and he pronounced it ye-ew. He said a
lot of words that were funny to Aidan and Doran, but the way he
said 'you' was always Aidan's favorite. On their walks back home
across country late at night, they held contests to see who could do
the best impression of MacGregor's accent. Aidan always won of
course, because he was around him the most and had developed a

natural miniature Scottish twang of his own anyways. Doran, who was always good and drunk by the time they left the old man's house, was much funnier to hear though, because he'd slur his over emphasized Scottish accent. There's no explaining it really except to say that it was funnier than all get out.

"We'll be sick for a month if we try to eat all of those. Maybe we should give some to..." Aidan was cut short by the old Scot.

"Whoa lad! We'll give them to no one! I know just what we'll do," he said smiling, with wide, hungry eyes, staring at the mushrooms, "We'll dry what we don't want to eat and then string em' up and hang em' in the root cellar just like they was peppers or the like. Then come winter, we'll use em' in our stews and have em' with our haggis!"

Even in the exuberance of the moment and in light of the glorious-ness of the day, Aidan winced at the very word *haggis*. It was the most God awful thing he'd ever heard of, let alone eaten. It came from the sheep, an animal not fit to feed to man, nor beast anyways. Then he'd take a bunch of the stuff out of them he called the pluck, but was really just heart and lungs and liver and such and then cram it all (along with a bunch of other stuff) into the very same animal's stomach. The resulting meal was one that tasted as bad, or worse, than it smelled even. The boys had always pretended to like it, and for his part, MacGregor never seemed to put the puzzle together of why his dog had a belly ache for an entire week every time he made the stuff. By then, however, even the mention of the word 'haggis' and Aidan's stomach began to turn as his mouth filled with the taste of his own bile.

"That sounds great, MacGregor," he replied. "Oh yeah, and I need to take a few hours off tomorrow starting around noon."

"Well, what are you telling me for?" the old man replied.

"Because I wanted to make sure you didn't pay me while I was off doin' other stuff is all," Aidan said.

"Pay you? I don't hardly pay you at all lad! Why, you'd be a Rockefeller by now if I'd paid you for every hour you've worked," MacGregor replied.

"I'll be off for a spell around noon anyways," Aidan said.

"Fine, that's just fine boy. I tell you what then," he said, in the kind of thoughtful talk that only MacGregor had, where his eyes squinted and he leaned toward you seriously while he spoke, as if this one conversation might decide the fate of all humanity. "First thing come morning, we'll go back to your secret spot and pick the rest of them mushrooms. Then when it's time for you to go, I'll come back here and start stringin' em up to hang and get all dried out."

About that time, Aidan heard Doran's voice calling from the field behind them. Doran and MacGregor loved each other's company. They had a very similar sense of humor and both enjoyed talking about crops and the weather and such. But more than anything, most of all, they both had a love for the drink. Three or four nights a week Doran would high tail it over to MacGregor's before Aidan could get gone and the three would sit into the wee hours of the night drinking.

Aidan liked to drink some as well, but nothing like the other two. Some nights he might not even drink at all. Either way, he loved the cool evenings spent sitting around warm fires under the starlit nights. He loved sitting and watching the clouds pass under the light of the moon. Even more than any of that though, he loved to just sit, listening to MacGregor and Doran. They were the funniest pair that Aidan had ever heard. He always said that they should get their own traveling show. They could go from town to town charging two bits for folks to sit and listen to them. Even when they argued, it was hilarious.

This night however, Aidan wished that Doran hadn't come. He felt like he had to stick around with them whenever Doran came. Aidan didn't feel like drinking or even sitting and listening to them. He had only wanted to go and be off alone. He had wanted to sit by himself, look at the stars and think of Maizey. He wanted to clear his head and figure out what he would say to her the following day. He wanted to dream of yellow dresses and voluptuous calves and tiny chocolate drops in emerald eyes.

He would think of those things, of course. Only he'd do it beside a fire with the drunks. At least they were funny, he thought, and turned back to the two talking of mushrooms and distilled mash.

Chapter 25   Dutch Pajamas

Even as Aidan sat by the fire half-heartedly listening to the two exchange stories he gazed off into the distance, admiring the moon shining brightly above him. He always stared in awe at the moon and the stars that filled the night sky. No matter how many times he sat outside in the country on a clear night, they never failed to take his breath away. Much in the same way, he thought, that *she* took his breath away...every time he looked at her.

Less than a half a mile away, down the road from where they sat, sprawled out upon a porch swing, Maizey lay gazing at the very same moon. Slowly rocking herself back and forth with a free leg pushing off of a porch column, Maizey stared at the dark moon valleys and wondered if somewhere, Aidan was looking too. She imagined that if they both looked long enough and thought hard enough that they both might be whisked away to the same far away crater in the moon, together and alone.

Maizey had not had much to do with boys, attending the all girl's Catholic school in Melrose. She didn't have any brothers her own age so boys were somewhat a mystery to her still. Sure, Tommy Flaherty had tried to steal a kiss around the corner from the five and dime last winter one Saturday night, but she hadn't felt anything for Tommy Flaherty. He'd only tried (and failed) because she had stolen away from her parents for a few moments to be one of the kids. Tommy had thought that she had done so specifically to be with him, but he soon learned his error. She'd turned straight away to rejoin her parents.

With Aidan it was different. It had always been different with Aidan. From the first time she laid eyes upon him years before when they were just kids, she knew that there was something special about him. She could tell when she looked into his blue eyes that he was not like the other boys. There was a soft kindness in them like she'd never seen before. He was just a dirt covered boy with messy hair like all the rest of them, but to Maizey, he was the most handsome boy she had ever set eyes upon.

Her father had said that Aidan was some sort of devil though, and she had never gone against her father's wishes before. Still, her father didn't *know* Aidan like she did. Even she knew that she didn't really *know* the boy. She also knew that try as she might, no one would ever understand or believe her. For she knew him better from looking into his eyes than if she'd known him for a hundred years. Her father didn't see what she saw in those eyes of Aidan's, he couldn't. If her father couldn't see what she saw, then how could he possibly *know* him? Aidan Keane a devil? Aidan was no devil. In fact, he was quite the opposite. To her, he was everything.

Years earlier, when Maizey was only eight or nine, the family had left their home in Northern Ohio to come to Iowa. They had done alright in Ohio, but her father had inherited a much larger spread in Iowa from a wealthy uncle. They had arrived just in time for a drought and plummeting prices to hit farmers all over the country.

Maizey had not made many friends in Iowa as her parents always doted over her and kept her by their side. In Ohio, she had been surrounded by cousins and friends and uncles and aunts. In Iowa, however, it had only been her, the sole child of an Irish Catholic couple who had believed that they could no longer conceive.

In a time when other families of their lot would be having eight, ten, or even twelve children, Maizey remained an only child for almost 16 years. That was, until her little brother Daniel had been born. Once he had arrived, everything changed in her life. She began to experience more and more freedoms that she had never known before.

That spring, the spring of 1933, her father's brother in Ohio had taken ill. Her father left them alone to return and care for his brother's stock and family. In his last letter, he had indicated that he may have to stay on quite a while longer. That was just fine by Maizey too, for while she missed her father and it meant that she was burdened with a lot more of the chores herself, it also meant that she would be able to get away more. It meant that finally, she would be able to see Aidan.

The following day began much like any other with her chores around the farm. Only on this day, Maizey hurried through all of them. Where before she might have walked slowly to gather eggs and feed the chickens and other stock, today she ran. Her mother had looked out the window and saw her running in sort of a funny half skip, half run and she could tell that today, more than most, Maizey was in very high spirits.

You could never tell with a girl that age, her mother had thought to herself. One day they would be sad and moping about aimlessly and cry at the drop of a hat. The next day they would be spry and smiling with a heart full of joy and laughter. No matter what the spirit, though, it was seemingly the result of absolutely nothing at all. It was only the age, she had thought, turning her attention back to her infant.

As Maizey hurried joyfully through her chores, she could only think of Aidan's eyes and the way they looked at her. No one had ever looked at her like that before. When he looked at her, she could feel the warmth of his very soul reaching out to touch her own. He moved her in ways that she had never imagined possible. When she looked up at him and found him gazing at her, she felt as though he were looking at the stars, so enamored was he. For the first time in her young life, she felt loved.

After completing her chores, Maizey ran inside the house and cleaned herself up as best she could. She was careful to wear a different dress than she had the day before too. She only had four dresses and Aidan would certainly see them all in due time. For now at least, she could create the impression of having more. She could, through her dresses, show him that she was the sort of girl who he might want to spend more time with. It was crazy to think of it that way, because clearly he felt something for her like none other, but still, she was nervous about her appearance and looking her best.

Finally, she told her mother that she was going to check on the cattle in the back lot. She didn't like lying to her mother, or to anyone else for that matter, but she knew that she would never be allowed to go if she told the truth. And she *had* to go. Nothing could keep her from it now.

Walking down the old country road, Maizey stopped several times to rub bits of dirt off of her shoes. She had discovered a wrinkle in the front of her dress as well, that she kept pushing down, in hopes that it might magically disappear. Looking up from such a pressing, she could finally see him standing there up ahead. He had just walked into the road near where they had last seen one another. It was the same spot where she had turned back to discover him still watching her walk away the day before. She imagined that he had never even left; that he had been standing in that very place all night awaiting her return.

As she neared she could see that his raggedy sandy blonde hair had been recently wet and pressed. It was still a mess, but there was clearly an attempt to groom it before their date. She smiled brightly as she approached. Boys were so funny, she had thought, even this one, they hadn't the slightest idea about such things as hair and caring for themselves. It was exactly this inability within them, she had reckoned, why every boy *needed* the right girl to take care of them.

"Hello Aidan Keane!" She said smiling brightly as she approached.

"Hello Maizey," he replied, trying to appear and remain stoic, but failing miserably and unleashing a huge smile of his own. "I've got you something," he said. With that he revealed his right hand that had been hidden behind his back. It was a small bouquet of spring flowers and little paper sack.

"Oh, Aidan," she said blushing, "I love those!" The flowers were called Dutchman's Breeches and he must've picked fifty of the tiny flowery stems. "Those are my favorites this time of year," she said, taking the flowers. It was true. She had always loved the way the tiny flowers looked like frilly upside down pajama bottoms. She supposed that the Dutch must wear pants like those as the name of the flower inferred, but she had never met a Dutchman as far as she knew. "Thank you," she said.

"Your welcome," he replied, "and I also made you some of these," he said, opening the sack to reveal a small batch of morel mushrooms, crisped up and cooked with spring onions.

"Oh my!" She said, reaching into the bag to sample one of the mushrooms. They were wonderful too. She loved the mushrooms and had never had them cooked quite that way before. "They're delicious," she said.

Just then, Maizey gasped as two heads appeared from behind the small hillside just on the other side of the fence that followed the road.

"Where's my mushrooms lad? You didn't make any for us?" MacGregor shouted.

"Yeah and where are my flowers?" Doran followed.

The two were holding the burlap sack that Aidan had used to gather mushrooms the day before. They had spent the night with MacGregor again, and as it was noon, the effects of their mid-week drinking binge had apparently subsided enough for them to return to the spot that Aidan had told them about. They stood together on the far side of the fence, Doran leaning on MacGregor's shoulder, and both of them proud and smiling.

Aidan cringed and turned beet red at the sound of their voices, "Don't mind them, Maizey. They must've got loose from the barn again. I'll tend to them later," he said, "They'll be safe there inside that fence." With that he grabbed her by the arm and began to lead her further on down the road toward MacGregor's house.

"Aren't you even going to introduce us?" MacGregor asked.

"Yeah," followed Doran.

"Later," Aidan said dryly.

"I'm Maizey," she yelled back over her shoulder to the two who stood watching them walk away. "It's a pleasure to meet you both."

"The pleasure's all ours," yelled MacGregor, and with that, the exchange had ended. The two drunks turned their attention back to the work at hand and began formulating a plan to corral the remaining mushrooms spread out before them.

"They're funny," Maizey said, smiling at Aidan.

"You have no idea," Aidan replied.

The two spent the rest of the afternoon together in MacGregor's back yard. It was there that Aidan told her everything. He told her about the dump and about going to school in Melrose as a dreaded yellow shirt. He told her about his father and his grandfather and the mother he had left behind. And he told her how through it all, she had been with him. That it had been her and her alone that had been there to see him through his most troubled of times.

When he had finished telling her everything there was to tell, the afternoon had passed them by like a motorcar on a busy lane. "That's how I know," he said, turning to find Maizey with tears streaming down her cheeks.

"That's how you know what?" she replied, looking into his eyes and feeling all of the pain that he had endured.

"That's how I know that I love you," he said. "Always have. Always will," he continued, "Always."

"Ooooooh," she cried, making her oh into a whining sound as she spoke it, "You're wonderful," she said. With that, she leaned in close to him. The nervousness of being so close melted away from her body as she stared into his kind, soft, blue eyes.

"Tiny little drops of chocolate," he said, "The left eye with twice as much," he continued, referring to the tiny little droplets of chocolate color in the tops of her otherwise green eyes. "They are so beautiful, Maizey...I..."

"Shut up," she said, and leaned in and kissed him. He was a tall, rough, messy boy. As messy as any she had ever seen. Everything about him was rough and rugged except for the softness in his eyes. Even his eyes, she discovered, weren't nearly as soft as the kiss of his tender lips though.

What precious little remained of the afternoon was melted away gazing into one another's eyes, giggling, smiling, laughing, and crying in a warm spring embrace. It was a day that neither of them would ever forget. Always.

Chapter 26   Summer 1933

In nearly everyone's life there is that one seemingly perfect summer. It is *the* summer that you look back on until the day that you die. The summer of 1933 was just such a one for Aidan and Maizey.

In the mornings, they both worked voraciously, tending to their chores and workloads as if they were the most urgent tasks ever assigned a body here on this Earth. The afternoons, however, belonged to them. The fields, ponds, trees and flowers all existed to please *their* senses and provide a back drop of eternal beauty to the love story that was unfolding between them.

Each day brought with it new adventures as they explored the world around them as if for the first time, together. For together, they could lay in a field and watch the clouds roll by or stop and examine the intricacies of a Tiger Lilly as if they had never before seen these things before. Through the eyes of love, they viewed the simplest of things, and the simplest of things brought them pleasure because they were together.

When alone, those same simple things viewed during the afternoon became symbols of the other to each of them. Aidan could pick a Tiger Lilly, or Maizey could stare at a cloud, and even though they were apart, it was as if they could see the other in the things that they had rediscovered together.

It was during one such afternoon late in August that the two were embraced and kissing in one of MacGregor's sprawling hayfields. It

129

was shortly after a leisurely swim in a nearby spring fed pond, that the two lay drying in the warm afternoon sun.

"Aidan," she said, turning to look him in the eyes, "I have something I have to tell you."

"What is it?" he asked. He knew the tone. It was the baring of bad tidings tone, like the one she had used a few weeks before when she wouldn't be able to see him the following day. Her mother had made plans for them all to go to Chariton for something or the other that day and there had been no way for her to get out of going along. It had killed him the entire day she was gone, not being able to see her, to hold her, to kiss her. It seemed to him now, more than ever, that without the warmth of her smile and without getting to gaze into her beautiful green eyes and admire the droplets of chocolate that he would surely fall over and die.

"It's my father, Aidan," she said, looking away from him sadly. "He's, he's coming back in a few days..." and with that tears began to well up in her eyes. It killed him inside to see those beautiful eyes ever well up with tears other than the tears of joy she had shed on so many days that summer as he whispered sweet things into her ear.

"Oh, Maizey," he said reassuringly, "It will be alright. You'll see. In time he will..."

"No," she cut him off abruptly, "you don't understand. He's coming back to get us. He is taking us all back to Ohio. His brother has died." And with that she broke into full fledge tears.

Aidan's heart sank into his stomach. He seemed to struggle for not only words, but the air he needed to breathe to even begin to form them. He felt nauseous, as if he would be sick right that very moment, and his head flushed beat red and broke into a sweat. She was his, by God. She was his now and no one would stand between them. He could not live without her, not any more, not after their summer together and finally holding her in his arms. How could he?

"Run away with me," he said without thinking. Even as the words flowed from his mouth, he struggled to envision what they would do or where they would go. He had been lucky in the summer of 1933 to even be employed by an old farmer who only paid him in mutton meat. Most boys his age did not have such a luxury that year. Hell, most adults didn't have such a luxury.

"Where will we go?" She asked him, turning back to look into his eyes to see if he wasn't fooling with her.

"I don't know yet," he replied, "but I love you Maizey. I love you like no one has ever loved another. I can't even begin to imagine living without you, love. You are the love of my life. No. You are more than that," he said, "You are my angel sent straight down from heaven. I need you like a body needs air to breathe or water to live. I love you."

"I love you too," she said sobbing, and held him tighter and closer than she had ever held anyone before, Aidan included.

"When is he coming home?" He asked, referring to her father.

"He will be home in a few days. We are to leave in two weeks time from today. He has arranged for neighbors to care for the Ohio spread only until then," she said.

Aidan had marveled all through the summer days at how life can be so cruel at times only to lead you into a perfect happy meadow, then right back out again. It was a perfect summer. The afternoons had been spent with Maizey, and the evenings were whiled away with MacGregor and Doran. It was as perfect a time as he had ever had in his life, and for if only a while he was happy. No, he was more than happy. He had thought that things would always be like that. He had almost begun to believe that the hard times of his life were but a distant memory.

Aidan had begun to think that life could be beautiful and perfect and wonderful as if in a dream. It had been a dream that summer; a beautiful, perfect dream. It would be etched into his memory as if it had been carved into marble. But soon he would learn for certain that life is not a dream and nothing that wonderful is meant to just be. Such times, such moments are much more like shooting stars;

amazing to behold and some are bright and colorful and memorable, but all of them fade as they plummet to the Earth. Soon, the dream, and his life, would all come crashing down around him into a thousand, tiny, broken pieces.

Chapter 27   Fond Farewell

That night, as Doran and MacGregor joked around their fire pit, Aidan stood off by himself, alone and staring at the night sky. He wondered how the sky could remain so beautiful despite all of the heartache that it witnessed beneath it. They were the same stars that he had looked at every night, all summer long, and dreamed of seeing Maizey. Now, however, they were different. They were still beautiful, but somehow different.

"What's wrong little brother," Doran called from the fire. The two had been experimenting that night with a new batch of rot gut that Doran had made himself using grandfather's revitalized still.

"Must be love troubles," MacGregor scoffed. "Aye. Love troubles. I've known them well myself, lad."

Aidan choked back his tears as he turned toward the two and began to speak. "Maizey's father is coming home soon. He plans to take them back to Ohio with him. I'm going to take her and run away." There, it was out.

"That is fool's talk lad," MacGregor spoke seriously. It was rare that he genuinely spoke seriously, but when he did, he commanded attention and respect from anyone in ear shot. "There is a depression going out there in the world. You've no idea what evils await two young people out there now. Take her to Missouri and get married if you like, then come back home."

"Yes. That is sound advice," Doran replied, "Listen to MacGregor."

"No," Aidan blurted. "Melrose is not my home. My home is wherever Maizey and I go together. Her father will never allow her to marry me, and if I try to steal her away, he'll have every Catholic lawman in the state out to do me in. No. We've got to leave here. There's no other way."

Doran stared back into the fire. MacGregor, however, rose and walked over to Aidan. He stood behind the young man and placed his hand upon Aidan's shoulder, "Whit's fur ye'll no go by ye!" he said softly.

"What is that?" Aidan asked softly, still staring off into the endless night sky.

"It means that what's meant to happen will happen, lad." MacGregor said softly, in almost a whisper. "I don't hold sway in such nonsense, but I think that you and she were meant to be one. Sure as anything I have ever known."

He could never tell if MacGregor said things like that because he truly believed them, or if he only said them because he cared so much about him. No matter why he said them, Aidan was glad that he did. It gave him not only comfort, but also a confidence that he was doing the right thing by Maizey. She would be his and his alone to take care of now. With only the thought of it alone, he began to mature inside, feeling the true pressure of being a man, the weight of responsibility for others.

The next morning began not unlike any other for Aidan. He and Doran had staggered home the night before. Aidan's announcement had set a somber mood over the fire and the two could not bring themselves to a good laughing drunk in his midst. As a result they had quit at a respectable hour, so all parties had decided to head off for their own beds.

Aidan had walked the fencerows back to MacGregor's house the following morning. He was careful to steer clear of the tall grassy fields where the morning dew would leave him soaking wet. When the dew soaked you good, it might be hours until the moisture could be replaced by your own sweat and chaffing was the only certain result of such a day. By this time of the year though, he and Doran alone, had created well worn footpaths along the fencerows on the cross country route between their two homes.

When he arrived at MacGregor's to begin his chores, he was greeted by MacGregor himself, up earlier than normal, and already bathed and primped for his day. Usually at that time of morning MacGregor, albeit awake, was a mess, staggering about in his soiled clothes from the night before. But this morning was clearly different and MacGregor even offered him coffee and bacon that he'd been cooking over his fire pit.

"I wish that I had a good yearling lamb's bacon to offer you lad, but I could only find this here hog meat. Filthy animals," he said, smiling slightly and looking at Aidan out of the corner of his eye as he stoked the fire. He knew that bacon was Aidan's favorite and he watched to see the boy look in awe at a Scotsman cooking meat other than god damned mutton, as the boys lovingly referred to it.

"What the hell has gotten into you?" Aidan replied, smiling. He recognized the importance of the gesture in the bacon. He knew that MacGregor had to have traded for it special as he never had once soiled his ground with a hog.

After eating the bacon and drinking a cup of coffee, Aidan stood to begin his chores for the day. As he did, MacGregor stopped him. "Wait, lad. There's something I want to show you. Just over this way," MacGregor stood and motioned him toward the house. The two walked together around to the far side of the old one story home and on past to a small shed on the south side of it. Aidan had always assumed that it was empty, and as he had no call to go snooping on an old Scotsman, he had honestly never bothered to peer inside the thing.

MacGregor reached down and pulled open the door to the small outbuilding. There, before Aidan's eyes was a 1926 Chevrolet Touring car. "Be damned," Aidan said with his jaw set wide open, "Why you old son of a..."

"Damn your tongue boy," MacGregor quipped, "You'd ought to know better than to curse in front of a lady." He said, admiring the car.

"She's beautiful," Aidan said, stepping into the building and admiring the shiny green sidewalls.

"She's yours," MacGregor replied. "I have no use for her these days. The top comes down and she goes like the wind. But I'm in no hurry to get to where I'm going, lad. Only off to meet my maker these days, and that day will come soon enough!" MacGregor smiled. He always smiled when he talked about "meeting his maker" as if he tempted fate and smiled into the very face of the death that awaited him.

"It's too much, Mac," Aidan replied. "I couldn't..."

"Nonsense, boy," MacGregor cut him off, "You've earned it and another one just like it. I've kept mark of every hour you've worked for me and you've more than plenty paid it off."

"I don't know what to say," Aidan stated, staring at the car and touching the cold, sleek steel panel along the door.

"Nothing to say, Lad," MacGregor replied. "It's shined and polished and full of gas for ya. Now take it and git. Yer employment is hereby terminated."

Aidan turned to the old man and saw a tear in his squinting eye. He walked over and hugged him. He had never hugged a man before that day. But he hugged old MacGregor sure enough.

"Go on now, boy," MacGregor said, trying not to show that he could no longer hold back his tears.

"Thank you, Mac," He said opening the door. "I'll never forget this."

Aidan slid behind the wheel and the engine fired right up. It idled like a dream. Slipping it into first gear, he let the powerful motor idle him out of the garage and on to the road, then felt it power up as he drove away, watching MacGregor through the growing cloud of dust behind him until he was gone.

Chapter 28   The Last Supper

That day around noon, Maizey left her house like every other. She hurriedly walked down the road to meet with Aidan at the corner post. She was wrought with worry on this day though, and her pace reflected it with short, quick steps. As she neared the post where they always met, she didn't see Aidan there. He was always there.

Just then from behind her, somewhere off in the distance, she heard the roar of the engine as the car accelerated toward her. She turned to watch as it passed and stepped well off the road to avoid the inevitable cloud of dust as it settled on her clean dress. But the car did not roar on passed her. Instead it slowed to a stop alongside her, and the driver leaned over and threw open the passenger door.

"Get in," Aidan said smiling.

"Aidan Keane," she stated abruptly, "you take this automobile back to where you stole it from immediately!"

"It's mine," he replied. "It's ours," he said, correcting himself. "Just get in Maizey. I'll explain it all while we drive."

Maizey climbed into the car and they sped on down the lane. Nearby, a Scotsman was climbing on his tractor when he heard the familiar sound of the purring engine. Smiling, he shook his head as he climbed on up and began singing an old Scottish tune to himself.

Aidan could see by her fidgeting that Maizey was nervous about *something*. He didn't ask though because he figured with their plans to leave and him showing up in a car, that it was all a lot for her to digest. He had decided just to let her be about the time she broke through the silence and began to speak.

"Aidan," she said turning to face him in the seat. He turned for a few seconds and looked into her eyes. He loved those eyes. To him they were like looking at the moon and the stars and all things beautiful all rolled up into one with tiny drops of chocolate in them, the left one twice as much as the right. "There's something I have to tell you."

"What is it?" He asked.

"I'm not leaving in a week or even two," she said. "My father is back. He had wanted to surprise my mother. He is planning on us moving tomorrow afternoon! He says the farm in Ohio can't wait. Oh, my God. I'm so sorry." She wept.

Aidan tensed as he heard the news, but it was no matter to him. They would simply leave a few days early. There were some things that he had wanted to do before they left, but none of them mattered as much as them being together. "We'll leave tomorrow round noon then, love," he said calmly.

"Noon?" She replied.

"Yes. Noon. Meet me at our spot at noon," he answered, "same as always. You had best leave a letter for your folks or something so they don't figure you for dead or the like."

"I will," she replied. Was she really going to do it? It seemed so rash and crazy and out of character to her. Could she be the type of girl that just ran off like that with a boy? She turned in her seat and looked at Aidan's face again, hair blowing in the wind and behind the wheel of the convertible as it sped down the road. As if on cue, he turned and smiled at her, gazing into her eyes. Yes. She absolutely was going to do it, she thought to herself. She couldn't live with herself if she didn't.

That afternoon did not afford them the same luxuries of the other days that summer. There was no time for laying about, holding one another and kissing. This day was reserved for tension and fear of the unknown and the stresses of the world more commonly reserved for adults. But it was agreed. They would meet at the corner post the next day at noon and begin their journey into the unknown and their new life together.

That evening, Aidan arrived home to find his brother waiting for him. As he walked into the small cabin they both shared as their living space, Aidan noticed that something was very different about the place. "Been cleaning?" He asked.

"Sort of," Doran replied. "I hauled some of my old junk I had laying around here to town and sold it. I got forty dollars all told. Brother, I want you to have it."

"Your treasures," Aidan said stunned as he looked around the room again, this time realizing that all of the old trinkets and collectibles and whatnots that Doran had salvaged and claimed as his own 'treasures' over the years were gone. He had always made fun of him for keeping it all and even cursed him when he'd stub his toe or bust his shin at night on them, but to Doran, it was all treasure. Every single piece of it a treasure with a story, and Doran had sold it all. "My god, Doran," he said as tears began to well up in his eyes.

"Take it brother," he said, handing him the pile of bills. "It's all that I can give you."

"Oh my God, Doran," Aidan said as the tears passed down his cheeks. With that Aidan engaged in his second hug of the day and his young life, with his brother in the living room of the shanty house.

"Now, let's go celebrate!" Doran wiped his cheeks and sniffled once, then grabbed a bottle as he headed toward the door. "You ain't leaving this God damned county until you've give me a ride in that car of yours!"

With that, the brothers drove away, off to MacGregor's for one last time as a trio. Aidan was comforted to know that the two would always have each other at least, his brother and MacGregor. He had never really fit in with them late at night as part of the act, but had served them well as an audience for their ongoing drunken antics. Aidan favored the drink on some nights, but far more often, he might only have a nip here and there, preferring just to sit quietly and watch the stars, listening to the other two as their tales grew taller with each gulp.

At MacGregor's that night, they were treated to mutton loin chops cooked over the fire pit. Done right, the way MacGregor done it, the loin was almost like not even eating lamb at all. It sort of even resembled a lean calf. Done wrong, the way that Aidan and Doran had tried to cook it in previous years, it was just as bad as the worst cut of front shoulder off of a lamb. Tough as nails and gamey as the oldest buck that ever lived.

The three imbibed on lamb chops and an old original batch of grandpa's own rot gut that Doran had saved for a special occasion. Aidan knew that he was experiencing something special with the two that night. He laughed more than normal with them, checking his pocket periodically to make sure the forty dollars was still safely tucked away. He drank more than normal too. As the evening wore on and the fire grew dim, it was he for a change who would stumble about telling taller tales than the other two.

Finally, with even the embers of the fire beginning to fade to black, and as the first hints of yellows and oranges began to dance on the night sky in the eastern horizon, they called it a night. Doran and Aidan held one another upright and staggered off toward the car. MacGregor wished them both one last farewell, and the two drove off from what would ultimately be the last time they would all three be together.

Chapter 29   Change of Plans

Maizey wrote a nice note to her parents. She had told them that the two were in love, and that Aidan was a kind heart and a kindred soul and that they needn't worry. She told them that she would write to them as soon as they were married proper and settled somewhere they could call home. She ended with a message of her love for them both and a request for their forgiveness. Then she had turned away, throwing her small bag outside the window and walking out to the yard to collect it.

Once again Aidan, twice for the first times ever and in the same two day period, was late. Maizey had moved her bag off the road so no one would be able to see it from up the way. She stood pacing nervously as the minutes ticked slowly past. She chewed on her nail and wondered where he could be. She always chewed on her nails when she was really nervous about something. It was a terrible habit sure enough, but there were times in her life that it simply couldn't be helped. These last few days had provided her with plenty such times.

She continued to pace until she finally heard a car rumbling from off in the distance. She stepped out from behind the bush and into the road to watch him as he approached.

WHAAAACK!

Maizey grasped her face and fell to the ground trying to make sense out of what had just happened to her. She clung to the horrible stinging pain in her face and tried to support herself out of the dirt with her free hand.

"Runnin' away are ya?" her heart sank deep into her chest and she thought she would be sick right then and there at the sound of her father's voice. "You'll do no such thing, you little whore, ya." He grabbed a handful of her hair and began to drag her down the road.

Maizey struggled to keep up with her hair as she could feel it pulling from the roots. Lurching ahead she stumbled to her feet and began walking sideways along behind her father. She knew even then, though, that her salvation was at hand as she heard the car slow beside them. She turned to look to Aidan as she heard the car slow almost to a stop. But even as she turned to look, the car and its' gawking driver only sped up and drove away into the distance.

He hadn't shown. Her knight did not ride in on a white horse or even drive up in his car. He had left her there. Her father had found her note and it was all over. She wept even as she continued to stagger down the edge of the road, struggling to keep up with her own hair as it tugged her forward in fits and starts. She wept, not in pain, but for the loss of a love that she could never replace, and she wondered if any of it was ever even real.

Chapter 30   6 Hours Earlier

Six hours before Maizey had been beaten down by her own father and dragged along the road by her hair, Aidan and Doran had sat watching the beautiful hues of the early morning sky from the hill in the Melrose Catholic Cemetery. They had stopped for only a moment or two to relieve themselves and finish off the last of a bottle, admiring the sky while they continued to talk about days long gone and those to come. '

Mostly, Doran talked about the car. He was in love with it. As they pulled out of the cemetery and headed back to the west toward their home, Doran rose in his seat and let the wind pass through his hair. "This is the God damnedest car I've ever seen!" he said.

The clickety clack of the shale road passed beneath them and even as Aidan reached to pull him back into his seat, he heard the explosion. It sounded as if someone had fired a shotgun right there inside the car. It was followed by the thud, thud, thud, of a blown tire. The impact from Aidan hitting the brakes had nearly landed Doran on the hood before slamming him squarely back into his seat.

"God damned shale," Aidan said, cursing the sharp rocks that were commonly used to gravel the roads of the time. He must have cut both foot and leg a dozen times on the sharp as glass busted shit and now, here he sat with a cut tire as well.

"God damn shale," Doran announced as if reading a king's proclamation as he tossed the empty bottle into the nearby ditch.

The two got out and learned the slow, hard way where the jack and spare tire were and how to use them. Doran was better at it than Aidan having worked in a junk yard for a hundred years, but he was of little practical use at the time due to his drunken state.

After nearly an hour, the tire was changed and they were finally headed for home.

"I love this god damned car," Doran said smiling as they sped down the road.

"I know you do brother," Aidan replied, "So do I!" He said and they both pushed back into their seats as he pressed down on the accelerator.

Doran stood up once again and threw his hands into the air. This time he was standing fully upright in the convertible and the wind passed over his entire face. "It's like I'm running a hundred miles an hour!" He announced. "Aaaaaaugh!" Doran let loose a primordial scream that he was certain could be heard on the moon.

"Aaaaaaaaaaaagh!" Aidan screamed, joining him in cadence and standing in his seat as well. It was a wonderful feeling, he'd thought, feeling the wind and the world speed by you. This was what freedom was like. Finally, after all of these years of watching trucks and trains pass by. This was it. "Aaaaaaaugh!..."

Aidan didn't see the small washout that ran into the road. He couldn't have seen it. Even if he hadn't been standing up with his brother, it probably wouldn't have made a difference. He would never know though. No one knows how far the car flew when it hit for sure, or how many times it rolled. When he landed Aidan looked up at the early morning sky and tried to think. "Doran," he said softly in almost a whisper even as the world around him faded into darkness.

Chapter 31   Rude Awakening

Seemingly just as the sky had faded, it lit up again. This time, though, Aidan found himself standing in a particular field where he and Maizey spent so much time that summer. It was bright and filled with flowers. In the distance the familiar silhouette of Maizey in a sun dress, ran toward him smiling. As she grew near, the sun became brighter and everything around him, including Maizey herself faded up into a blinding white light.

Aidan opened his eyes and looked at the blurry figure standing over him. "Maizey," he whispered softly. Just then he was hit with horrible pain throughout his body, It struck him as if he had been struck by a fast moving train and he moaned out loud.

"No lad," the reply came. "It's me, MacGregor." The figure replied to him softly.

"Where is Maizey?" He asked, trying to focus on the figure in front of him.

"She's gone lad. Gone away with her family," he replied. "Don't you fret about that now, lad. We've got to get you better. We thought you were dead for certain."

"What?" Aidan said, trying to figure out what had happened and where he was. "Where is Maizey? Where the hell am I?" Aidan got angry and tried to sit up, but pain shot through his spine and radiated out to every conceivable nook and cranny throughout his body.

146

"You're in the hospital," MacGregor replied. "You were in an accident. Now, just you lay back and rest, lad."

"Where's Doran?" Aidan asked, still annoyed and angry at the situation, but not willing to risk another painful attempt at sitting up. He waited for an answer to come, but it never did. The silence rang out throughout the room and filled Aidan's ears like a scream. "What about Doran?" He asked again.

"He's gone lad," the reply came. "He's passed on."

"Oh God," Aidan cried, "Doran." He wept silently having talked enough. Everything was gone. All was lost. There was nothing left but the pain, both inside and out.

MacGregor stood over him day and night for eight days while Aidan lay unconscious. The doctors had said there was almost nothing they could do for him and that he was as good as dead. That was eight days before. He had laid there bleeding and dying for hours along that lonely stretch of road before anyone even found them. It took hours more to get him to Chariton to the hospital.

MacGregor had come to watch his friend die. He couldn't allow him to die alone. Aidan had been like a son to him, Doran too. He had wanted to be there to lay Doran to rest as well, but he was only one man and this world is for the living first. Besides, Aidan had been alone enough in his short life; he wouldn't have him dying that way too.

But that had been eight long days before. Each day, he watched young Aidan dance with the devil and fight off death. He was a fighter, that one. He had known a hundred other men who would have just slipped quietly away, but not Aidan. He wasn't going anywhere without a fight, not even there.

The winter of 1933-34 was one of the harshest on record. Snow drifted the roads fuller than anyone could remember seeing them and the winds howled almost nonstop. Aidan had spent the entire winter recuperating at MacGregor's house. Barely able to move at first, he came to rely upon the old man for all of his most basic needs. MacGregor, to his credit, cared for Aidan as if he were his very own son through it all.

By the time the snow finally melted away, Aidan was able to walk unassisted. He would do so with a considerable limp though. Time would heal the leg and the limp would get progressively better, but he would have it in some form or another until the day that he died.

Some wounds, however, do not heal so easily, and not a day could pass him by without long periods of quiet sobbing for Doran and Maizey. He would cry until there were no more tears to cry, at times for one, at times for the other, and at times for both. Then he would sit and stare blankly out the window until his body alerted him of its ability to produce tears once again.

Losing Maizey was more than he could have taken all by itself. But to have killed his own brother (and there was no mistaking it no matter what MacGregor said, he *had* killed his own brother), it was more than he could endure. He had never believed the stories before then, but they were true, sure enough. He and his entire lot were cursed. They *were* the devils of the dump; heathens born only to suffer and bring suffering unto others.

By spring, MacGregor would have had to hide his guns and Scottish daggers, as well as anything else that Aidan spent too much time studying. Indeed, there were many days that year when MacGregor returned back to the house from chores and was actually surprised to find the boy still alive. He was a fighter, that one. Always.

Chapter 32   Summer 1934

Aidan was finally able to be up and walking about. He had barely survived the winter with his life though; sitting in the house and watching the four walls fill with ghosts slowly close in around him. He tried, as much as he could, to stay drunk at the urging of MacGregor, who was constantly trying to wash away his melancholy with the only medicine that the old man had ever known.

As the cool days slowly yielded to the heat of the summer, Aidan was able to walk farther every day. As the heat of summer came full on in July, he could walk all the way to Melrose. There he began gravitating toward the bars where men foolish enough to cross the young man who could barely walk were in for a huge surprise, as nothing in his injuries precluded him from delivering lightening quick blows. They landed at seemingly blinding speeds and brought more than one much older, larger man to his knees.

Indeed, most of Aidan's seventeenth year, like so many other years to come, would be spent in a tavern trying to drink away the ghosts. Quiet and quick fisted, he would sit, mostly staring into the mirror behind the bar, drinking and thinking of Doran, and of Maizey. Always Maizey was there, haunting his memory and driving him insane. He had killed his brother and there was no power in this world or the next that could change that, but somewhere, out there, Maizey might still be waiting for him...somewhere...in Ohio.

He didn't even know the name of the town she had moved to. He only knew that she was somewhere in the north part of Ohio. To him, a country boy from rural Monroe County, Iowa, it could have just as well been the moon itself. Pffft. Ohio.

He wasn't even sure where the state was any more. He had lost so much of his education in the accident. There were whole subjects that had simply slipped his mind, and the boy who once could read Latin could barely read in English now. The worst part of it was that he remembered that he used to know so much more. It would have been easier if he just could have forgotten altogether, all of it; Doran, Maizey, Melrose, all of it. Or better yet, if he had just died altogether.

Aidan had only just got to the Melrose Tavern for the fifth day in a row that week. He had just walked in and sat down. He had ordered a drink and as the bartender ambled down to the other end of the bar to pour it, Aidan sat studying himself in the mirror. How many hours had he wiled away in there at that very stool just looking in the mirror? How many days this month? Or the month before that one? What the hell was he doing?

Suddenly as the bartend turned toward him with his drink, he felt an urgency to get out of there. He felt boxed in and trapped and it was hard to breathe. He felt like if he didn't get up that he would still be there, sitting at that bar in a hundred years like the quiet old pickled mummies who lined the stools every day. Aidan turned for the door, but before he left, he turned and took one last look around, slugged down his whiskey and walked out into the early afternoon sun.

Walking down the little main street passed the businesses; Aidan turned south and headed toward the tracks. There he stood where the road intersected with the rails. He stared off into the distance to the West wondering what lay beyond the curves and straight ways that he had become so familiar with in his youth. Then he turned and stared at them in the other direction. He had been there long enough, he had thought. In that spot, wondering what lay in his path and in his future. He had worn out his welcome at MacGregor's, in the town and in his own skin. It was time.

'Head west young man, head west,' the words of Horace rang out in his ear from some unknown distant place in his memory. With that he turned back and faced the westward rail once again. As he took a step toward the tracks, he heard the screeching of brakes. The car skidded to a stop as it rounded the corner, nearly killing him where he stood. By the time it got to a complete stop the hood emblem was inches from his abdomen.

"Good God! I nearly killed you," the man said as he leaped out of the car. The man began to step toward him. As he did, his long, brown coat swept alongside the car, and he reached up, securing his matching brown fedora hat against the gust of warm wind that swept through the valley.

"That's alright," Aidan replied as he turned back toward the tracks to walk away.

"Wait," the man called out, stepping closer toward him. Then the stranger stopped short, to avoid the mud puddle along the roadside, a drying, dying remnant of a recent summer rain, "hold up."

Aidan swung round to face him again, one foot off the road. "Yeah?" He replied.

"You wouldn't happen to know how to drive a truck would ya?" The man asked, cocking one eyebrow upward and leaning in slightly toward him.

"Sure I do," Aidan replied, still with his right foot ahead of him facing toward his future.

"You lookin' for work?" The man called after him.

"Sure," Aidan replied. "Ain't everybody?"

"Hop in then! The name's Harris, Phil Harris, and we've got to get going!" The man said, turning about face and walking away even before receiving an answer. Without another word, he climbed back into his car and shut the door.

Aidan stopped and looked at the tracks once more. He wondered what lay beyond the handful of bends and miles that he was familiar with. 'Well,' he thought, 'you was looking for your future. I guess it come a lookin' for you too.' Then he turned and climbed into the car as it sped away.

Chapter 33   The Road

Five years had passed since that day when Brown had nearly run Aidan over with his Sedan. Five years since Aidan had been back to Melrose. It was 1939 and in a few months he would be turning 23 years old. That day, he had climbed into the cab of a truck filled with swinging beef at the Harris plant, driven away, and never looked back.

There were a thousand men in that county alone who would have killed to get the job, maybe more. Back in Chicago where he would deliver that first load, there were tens of thousands who would have literally killed to have it. Aidan got it because as luck would have it, Harris' workers had just finished loading the truck, owned by a specialty supplier in Chicago that catered to high end restaurants, when the driver had suffered a heart attack. He would die on his way to the hospital that very day too, in the backseat of Harris' Sedan.

He had been speeding on his way back from the hospital when Harris had nearly killed Aidan in the road. It was also, as Harris would recount in a hundred drunken stories between the two years later, what he considered to be a divine intervention, as he had yet to address the problem of what to do with the trailer full of beef and ice blocks destined for the windy city.

After a full day of hunting together, years later, Harris would lift his glass, smile, and recount how he had nearly run Aidan over. He would make exaggerated gestures with his hands to show how he got out of the car and the wind struck him in the face with dust, blinding him just long enough to offer such an important job to a mere child. But, by the time Aidan had climbed into his car, he was in such hurry, and such a bind, that he just said to hell with it and sent him on his way. "It wasn't my truck anyways," he'd say smiling wryly. "But I'd have never guessed in a million years that they'd keep him on in Chicago!"

It would turn out to be the longest drive of his young life, in miles AND stress. The box truck reacted to the gusting summer wind like a kite. But worse, far worse than that, was that all of the beef had been loaded on the hook, swinging in the box. That meant that every time he turned a corner, the beef turned the corner. Aidan could feel the tires lose their grip as the swinging weight would threaten to topple him. Likewise, when he slowed the truck, or God forbid, had to apply the brakes, the weight would shift forward and give the entire truck an extra push forward. It was a white knuckled drive to say the least.

The drive had been a slow one too. It had included dozens of stops for directions, but when he had arrived in Chicago with a safe load of swinging beef and a hastily scratched letter from Harris explaining the situation to them, they kept him on. When that supplier was bought up by a grocer, they kept him on too as a long-haul, specialty driver.

He had learned to love life on the road in that time. He had finally made it out of Melrose and he had sworn that he would never even go back to visit. He had sent word to MacGregor when he had first gone, and even sent a few funny post cards back to him from various places, but he hadn't fretted about leaving. They had talked about it quite a bit before he had gone, in fact.

MacGregor himself had told him how he was looking more and more like a bird ready to fly the nest at any moment. "Don't bother with good-byes when you're ready to go lad. We both know this ain't the place any more for you," he had said. Even five years later, as Aidan imagined his words, he smiled at the way MacGregor said 'Yeeew'.

Then, with half a decade in the rearview mirror, Aidan recalled the words of the man he was going to back to visit. He should have gone back before then or wrote more often, but theirs wasn't that kind of relationship. Their affections and adorations of one another had always gone largely unspoken. There was never any doubt in either of them though, that they were both the father and the son that the other had never had.

Aidan had tried to stop once to see MacGregor when he'd been through to pick up a load of beef from Harris' to the Southwest, near the Missouri border, but no one was about and iced beef only waits so long.

It had always perplexed him that Chicago, with their vast beef yards, millions of head of cattle, and hundreds of packing houses, would send him on sixteen hour round trips to pick up a single load of beef. But Harris beef was prized for being grain fed (a secret blend of corn and oats) and for never dirtying their hooves with the stench of the huge cattle yards. It was even said that some of it went directly to the owners of the yards and packing houses themselves, to be served at their private residences.

Whatever the case, Aidan had received everything that he could dream of out the arrangement. He drove all over the mid-west and even the East Coast for in-season berries and the like. Once, he even drove all the way to Maine for a load of Guinea birds. Guinea birds! He thought it was the damnedest thing, made even funnier when they had unloaded them in Chicago. He could tell that the bosses there had no idea what they had been doing when they had placed the order. Exactly how clueless they had been was only revealed when he arrived with his delivery. The birds made hellish noises and half of them flew the coupe and lit upon the rafters of the warehouse shitting all over dozens of crates of produce and other goods. Made even worse was the fact that the meat from the birds itself was a hue of purplish, blackened hell that proved to be impossible for *anyone* to market at a profit.

Aidan loved making the long runs, the freedom of the road, and even the people he met along the way. It wasn't that he ever managed to make friends of any of them, because the open road and different routes every week didn't lend itself to making any real friends. No, he loved the people because to them he was only another face in the crowd, another truck driver stopping for coffee and a bit of bacon. He was a random face in the crowd and they all treated him same as any other.

No one on the road ever once asked him his religion or where he came from or who his family was. Fact was, no one cared. That alone, which makes the road such a lonely place for so many people, was what he loved most about it.

There were a lot of other things that he loved about the work as well, like the long hours of thoughtful quiet. He could sit for hours, listening to the whir of the wheels on the road and think about life. He could have used the time to dwell on all that he had been through, but instead, his mind focused on the road ahead, the possibility of what might lay around the next bend, the next town, the next state.

Life was a lot like the road, he'd surmised, if you can hang on to the wheel long enough to get through the storms and the rough spots, eventually the sun would rise again, and you'd hit a stretch of new pavement. Of course, it always changed. The road, like life itself, was always changing and the good patches didn't last long either, but at least you knew they were out there; you just had to hang on and keep driving forward until you got to one.

He always looked to the road ahead of him and tried not to stop moving long enough to think about anything else. Even when he wasn't driving or sleeping, he would hang around the loading docks or help clean up the warehouse or work on his truck. It was the company's truck of course, but he cared for it like it was his own. It was largely because of that care that they had let him take it for the week back to Iowa. They had scheduled the pick up of a load from Harris' and told him to go a week early to pick it up.

Being based in Chicago, they had union rules to work by, and everyone had a certain amount of vacation time. Aidan had never taken any of his. Worried that the union would figure it out and cause trouble over it, his boss had told him that he would have to take *some* time off, *somewhere.* Since Aidan knew that he still owed it to MacGregor to visit, he agreed to spend a week back in Southern Iowa. He figured he could finally take Harris up on some fishing and quail hunting while he was in the area and kill two birds with one stone, so to speak.

Turning off of Highway 34, Aidan geared up as his truck rolled over the first hill then let it coast the downside. Just outside of town at the small farm on the East side of the road heading into Melrose, a young father stood outside in the yard, watching his children play. A mother emerged from the house carrying a pitcher and all of them stopped and waved as he passed slowly by. He smiled and waved back at them reading the Catholic name on the post by their drive.

It was finally over, he thought. Even here, he was just another face in the crowd, just another stranger, who if you bothered even to ask, was named Aidan. Without ever realizing that he was feeling anything else, or that the emotion had so moved him, Aidan reached up with his sleeve and wiped away an almost imperceptible tear from his rugged wind chaffed cheek.

Chapter 34   MacGregor's Last Gift

Slowing to a stop, Aidan pulled the truck off to the shoulder atop the hill just shy of the North edge of Melrose proper. He climbed down out of the truck and looked up at the warm afternoon sun that radiated down over the front of him. He had learned over the years to enjoy what each of the seasons had to offer him, and he stopped at every opportunity, even if for only a second, to soak in the best of each. The Sun, hot and shining and beaming, caused most to retreat into shade, praying for cooler days. For Aidan it was a moment to be savored though, and relived during some distant long, cold winter storm.

Aidan closed the door of his cab behind him and squinted down the hillside into the town below. It was, he decided, actually nice to see the familiar main street, lined with businesses and people out on their daily errands or just visiting with neighbors. Across the road, an old woman stood on a porch beating a rug and even she ceased for a moment to give a quick wave of the hand, an approval to the stranger that Melrose was open for business to him. No one here seemed at all to see the old faded yellow shirt of an outcast that had once adorned his body.

He turned away from her after returning the wave and a warm smile, and walked through the small gate along the roadside. Careful to watch his step, he inhaled the smell of fresh cut hay wafting from an adjacent field. The hay had always caused his nose to stop up almost

158

instantly, but still, he couldn't resist the smell and taking it in and remembering countless days spent filled with laughter on MacGregor's farm.

Stopping near fresh earth, he knelt down and picked up a small handful. Already there were blades of new green grass shooting up throughout it and he cleared them out of the dirt in his hand. To this day, he still had difficulty reading, but sorting the grass and sticks from the earth, he slowed his mind enough to read the etched words before him.

Ross C. MacGregor III
b.1878 Scotland
d.July 23,1939

Aidan smiled warmly and spoke to his old friend. "Well I will be damned," he said, "you made it to over sixty. It must have been all that mutton and whiskey."

He could almost hear his friend talking back to him too, making some witty comeback in his thickest of native drawls. MacGregor's brogue always thickened when he was being witty, and today, in Aidan's mind was no exception.

Aidan felt no sadness for the loss of his friend, in part because he had come to view death differently than most folks. To him, it had become a natural state and part of life itself, no more to be feared then going to sleep at night. He had no beliefs per say, and scoffed at the notion of organized religion, but there was no fear of death within him, and therefore, it was easier to accept the loss of a friend as well.

MacGregor, he had been told, had been done in by his own beloved tractor. How many times Aidan had warned him against standing while he drove the thing, but the old Scotsman had done things his own way his entire life. He would have none of it. In the end, he had fallen off, just as Aidan had predicted would happen, and been run over by his own disc. Aidan imagined that he had cursed in his last second, but only due to the thought of the lad being right and that he would stand over his grave and say 'I told you so.'

"I told you so," Aidan said, placing the handful of dirt into a small tin and shoving it into his pocket.

"What did you tell him?" The voice caused Aidan to jump and startle, even letting loose a funny sound like a dog that had just been nipped by another.

"You gave me quite a start," he said to the girl who was still laughing just a bit in her pride of having startled him so.

"I'm sorry," she replied, but clearly she wasn't really sorry at all. "How did you know him?" She asked.

"I used to work for him," Aidan replied. "He was my best friend. Did you know him?"

"Of course," she said, "he was my uncle. I mean I hadn't seen him since I was a little girl and I never really got to *know him,* know him, but he was my uncle."

As she spoke, Aidan could see what must have been the family twinkle in her eye. She had the MacGregor ornery, he reckoned. Kneeling down on her haunches, she placed a small bunch of fresh cut flowers on the earth in front of them. As she did so, Aidan admired her long, flowing, wavy dark auburn hair. She was long and slender and taller than most men of the day, and she had a deep, sultry voice like nothing he had ever heard before.

He had met a few different girls during his life on the road. The kind of girls that one meets on the road and enjoys spending time with, but doesn't bother you to leave when it's time to go. Not that they were homely girls, or anything particularly horrible about them either. There was just something very casual about meeting someone on the road. They were fun and fast and Aidan was a funny, handsome young man just passing through.

There was definitely something different about this girl, though. Maybe it was only because he was back in Melrose; maybe it was that she was MacGregor's niece. But something about her made his

160

heart quicken like it hadn't done in a very long time. Hell, not since Maizey had he felt anything close to that.

It had nearly killed him, losing her, but time has a way of changing our memories to protect us. From this distant place in the future, he could even imagine that his feelings weren't as strong as he had once imagined. He could look back and almost laugh at himself and his youth. What the hell would they have ever done anyways? And what the hell was MacGregor thinking giving him a car and lending aid to his youthful stupidity?

"What's your name?" The girl looked up at him, and for the first time he noticed her large, round, bright, beautiful hazel eyes. They were definitely a hazel mix of green and brown hues, but in the bright summer sun shining on her auburn hair, they seemed more of a greenish grey like the water at the beach of Lake Michigan.

"I'm Aidan," he replied.

"My name is Claire, Aidan," she said, rising while extending her hand out to him.

"Pleased to meet you, Claire," he said, shaking her hand. The two stood there for only a moment, locking eyes, and their hands remained embraced. It was as if they both knew there was *something* between them and neither wanted to let go. She had the longest fingers he had ever seen, and they took forever to gently slide out of his hand. Aidan had to swallow and clear his throat to hide his nervous tension as she withdrew.

"Do you have time?" She asked. "I'm certain my father will want to meet you. We are out at the farm now."

"Yes," he replied. "I have time. Would you like a ride out there?" he asked.

"Sure," she said. "I've never ridden in a big truck like that one before, but only if I can blow the horn in town."

"Deal!" He said enthusiastically. Yes. He definitely liked Claire. She was tall and pretty and funny and a little bit crazy and dangerous like her uncle had been.

Keeping with their bargain, she even blew the air horn as they passed through the main street. She kept on blowing it in quick successions and laughing all the way back to the MacGregor place, in fact. She really was lovely.

"Your uncle taught me to drive trucks," he yelled over the sound of the horn, but she only laughed, not hearing his words. So he gave up trying to say anything at all the rest of the way and only laughed along with her until they pulled into the drive.

Chapter 35   Chicago

Aidan couldn't have known it that day, but that winter, in the first days of 1940, only four months after they first had laid eyes upon one another, he would take Claire as his first, and only, wife. He still drove trucks out of Chicago, so he found them a small flat in the city. It was far enough away from the stockyards and the slums to be clean and safe for his wife and the child that was already on the way. It was more than he could afford forever on his salary, but he had saved quite a bit during his years of bachelorhood and constant working so he figured, why not *live* a little?

Most folks from the farm shrink in fear at the hustle and bustle of the city when they first arrive, but not Claire. For her, it was as an awakening to a world that she had never dreamed to have existed, but where she seemed to naturally belong. She was twenty-four when she moved there, and the fast life of a city girl suited her independent nature. She found in Chicago that women weren't just born unto this world to fetch eggs and cook and clean up after others. Chicago women did *everything* and the sky seemed to be the limit for them.

For Aidan, it was amazing to experience the world around him through her eyes. It was as if he was seeing things for the very first time. He saw so many things with her that he had never even noticed before. The architecture that filled the city's buildings, the bright lights of the city at night, even the way the shadows changed the colors of the city around them as the sun rose higher in the sky. She seemed to find beauty and wonder everywhere, and in everything, and he loved that about her.

For his part, Aidan gave up the lucrative over the road route, and took a position for the same company performing mostly local deliveries. He knew that if he and Claire were going to be truly happy together, that he would have to be closer to home. And besides, he wasn't much keen on the idea of leaving his beautiful young bride alone for weeks at a time in the city, or anywhere else for that matter.

In the morning, she would rise up before the sun and make them both breakfast. Then she would go for long walks by herself along the lakeshore or through the park. Some days she would visit an art museum or one of the many countless wonders that the city had to offer its' citizens. In the evening the two would dine out somewhere, usually at their favorite little local diner on the corner, Smithy's Place. The food was always divine and there was a lot of it.

Afterwards, they liked to take short walks around their own neighborhoods and watch the lights go on in the buildings all around them. It was almost like watching the stars at night back home it was so breath taking at times. Through her, Aidan could find the wonder in it all. Through her, he could finally find rest for his weary soul and happiness and a simple pleasure out of just living.

Aidan had always looked out on the open road and wondered what was *out there.* He had never imagined it being this good or this easy though. Claire was smart and bright eyed and pretty and funny and Chicago was their playground. Life was very good, and for the first time in his life, Aidan felt that he wasn't in such a hurry to get around that next bend. This stretch of road, he thought, could last the rest of his life. This straightaway could just keep right on going and it would be just fine with him.

But even as he lived it up and drank in the sweetness of the moments they shared together there in the windy city, he also knew deep in his heart that such stretches of road almost never last long. He knew deep inside that despite your best efforts, life always changed, the road always took a turn when you least expected it to.

One night walking with his new wife, he stopped and picked her up and looked into her eyes and just held her tightly. "I love you," he'd said, "more than anything, more than ever. Promise me that you'll never leave me alone. Promise me that it will be like this forever between us?" He said as he set her feet back on to the city sidewalk.

"I promise," she said smiling. "I love you too," she replied. "I am not ever going to leave you. I promise. Now stop talking that way. You're scaring the baby!"

She was funny that way. She loved to talk about the baby as if it was right there listening to everything they said. She knew that it really wasn't, of course, but she always said it anyways just to be funny. "You're scaring the baby by talking about the baby all the time," he replied. "I bet he thinks his mother is crazy by now!"

"You take that back," she demanded, "you're going to make the baby cry talking about her mother like that!" She also loved to insinuate that the baby was going to be a girl.

"Really?" Aidan replied cocking one eye brow upwards as he looked at her.

"Yes, really," she said succinctly.

"Well, it so happens that he already told me the other day that he thinks his mother *is* crazy as a loon," he said smiling.

"She did not!" She protested, "When?"

"While you were napping a few nights ago," Aidan replied slyly.

"Well," she said, "in that case, *she* will be in big trouble when she arrives, and since you two have been so busy conspiring against me already, *you* will get to change all of *her* diapers when *she* arrives!" And with that she made a gesture with her shoulders and walked faster, ahead of Aidan, leaving him alone to ponder the dirty diapers.

'God, I love her,' he had thought to himself as he ran to catch up, smiling at having been bested in another of their silly make believe arguments.

It was a wonderful time for both of them and the road that stretched out before him was smooth and straight and free. Secretly, for the first time in his life that he could remember, he prayed that it would last forever...even though he knew it never would.

Chapter 36   Alone in the Crowd

It was late in October of 1940, only days before Aidan's own 24th birthday when his son was born at Chicago's Provident Hospital. When the doctor came out and told him that he was the father of a son, Aidan stood patiently in line behind two other fathers to use one of the pay phones. It took for what seemed like forever to get to the phone. He had a list of her family he was supposed to call the minute he received word and knew that Claire was alright.

Stepping up to the phone, Aidan lit a cigarette and reached into his coat pocket for the list. Chicago was unseasonably cold in October compared to back home. They said it had something to do with being on the water as they were, but nonetheless, you had to start at least carrying a coat with you in mid September, lessen you get caught off guard by the rapidly changing weather and dropping temperatures. After all, they didn't call it the windy city for nothing.

Aidan turned as he placed the receiver to his ear and looked back across the waiting room. There was a constant and steady stream of men coming and going, pacing, and chain smoking in the little room and spilling in to the corridor. The white washed walls of their little nook were stained a dark yellow and dripping of tar from months of smoking. He figured they must have to white wash the walls in there at least three or four times a year to try to stay ahead of the tar. He thought momentarily that their time might be better spent putting in a bigger a window instead, and turned his attention toward the list.

To his left, on the other phone, a short, balding thirty-something stood teary eyed, talking to his father. He kept calling him 'pop' and unconsciously squeezing the form out of his fedora that he clutched tightly in his free hand. Aidan thought for a second about saying something to the guy to save his hat, but ultimately decided against it. What the hell did he care if the guy ruined his hat? It was *his* hat after all.

Scrolling down the list of names and phone numbers, he reached into his pocket and pulled out a large pile of coins he had brought along for just this occasion. He stacked them neatly atop the phone and readied himself to dial. As he finished stacking them, he searched the list once more for a first number to dial. As he did so, it hit him like a ton of bricks from above. It was Claire's list. It was all her list and hers' alone.

His mind's eye filled with images of his own father, his mother who had disappeared off the face of the earth some years before, MacGregor, Doran, even his Grandfather. There was no one left for him to call. The birth of his son was one of the largest events of his young life, and he had no one to call and tell about it.

He thought of his mother as she sat reading with him and teaching him things years before she began hitting the bottle, and before she had lost her mind. He remembered his father wanting him to have more out of life, wanting him to rise above their own family name and background. His mind then raced ahead to Doran and MacGregor as they all sat laughing around a fire pit. And he thought of Maizey, the drops of chocolate in those eyes as they stared back at him, beckoning his soul to follow her own to a distant place that both of them would recognize as home.

His heart sank into his stomach, and before he could dial the first number, he felt like he might pass out for lack of air. He struggled to catch a breath, but the smoke filled room only seemed to choke him further as the dripping yellow white washed walls closed in around him. He was alone, he thought. His heart ached with sadness and he struggled to keep his composure.

Aidan reached for the pile of coins to clear them from atop the phone, but he only knocked them to the floor. As coins hit and then rolled all across the floor, the movement of all of the pacing nervous men stopped. Aidan looked up from the coins, eyes filled with tears, and all eyes were upon him, staring at him as if he were some sad, strange circus attraction.

If only for a second, standing there, he was back in school, donning a puke yellow shirt, and standing in front of a cafeteria full of eyes as the Reverend Mother struck him from behind again, counting off and cursing him in a litany of religious epitaphs. Grabbing his chest, Aidan ran out of the room and down the hallway, knocking a man in a wheelchair into the wall. He kept running out the door and didn't stop until he was almost out of the parking lot.

"Leave me alone!" He screamed into the emptiness of the Chicago night. Bending to his knees, Aidan breathed in the clean, cool, fresh air. MacGregor had talked often of spirits. 'They're all around us,' he would say. They were ghosts of long gone spirits, yet to be born ones, and even some that never were or will be. He had never believed MacGregor's synopsis of being surrounded by spirits of any sort really, but he had definitely come to believe in ghosts. They weren't the sort that sailed around the room in old flour sacks either. Those he could have seen, and he could deal with anything that he could see. No, these ghosts were far worse; they existed only in his mind and they haunted him still, even now, years after he had hoped them to be long gone.

Often times, while he was on longer drives by himself, he still found himself talking aloud to his ghosts. Some of them he knew for a fact weren't real, like the Reverend Mother. He knew for a fact because the old hag was still very much alive and haunting the souls of Melrose even then. But others, like Doran and MacGregor, and even his own father, had never really left his mind after all and he filled countless miles talking to them.

Usually they existed only to keep him company and fill his time. Talking to them had given him comfort on his long drives. But every once in a great while, at times when he least expected it like this, they all came flooding back into his mind at once, and they reminded him, by their very existence, that in this world, he remained, completely alone.

Chapter 37   Merril's Last Wish

Looking into the bright, sparkling eyes of his newborn son, Aidan held him upright before him and named the boy in honor of two of his ghosts. Doran Merril Keane stared blankly out at the world the way babies do, trying to make sense of the flood of colors and shapes and smells and sounds all around them. To Aidan, looking in his son's eyes was like looking back into time through a million years of human evolution. It seemed that the baby had the wisdom of a thousand lifetimes in those eyes.

Claire's own mother would comment later that she felt that all babies had a sort of dumb look on their faces, but Aidan never thought so at all. He thought that they, more than any of us, held all of the secrets of the universe still, brought along with them from the great beyond from whence they had recently sprung. He reckoned that only time and their experience here on this earth made them forget all that they seemed to know, and grow into the person they would slowly become.

Aidan had thought it appropriate that his son should carry Doran's name. He didn't get the feeling that he *was* Doran, even though he believed the possibility might exist for such a thing to occur, but he felt that the name deserved the opportunity to at least have a full life, not one cut short as his own brother's had been.

As for the middle name Merril, he couldn't help but honor his father, if only to say that through this child, his dream had finally been fulfilled. The chain that bound his father's body and soul as a Devil of the Dump and heathen had been irreparably broken with the birth of this child in Chicago. His son would never even know all that had happened so far away in Melrose. Baby Doran would never even know the story of all their family had been through, let alone be forced to endure the stigma of being a despised outsider.

Claire had always wanted to name her first born a name from her own family, but they had also agreed in advance that the honors would go the one who guessed the sex of their baby. She never imagined it possible that her daughter might actually be a son, but she was far from disappointed. In short order though, she began to call the boy by the pet name of Dory, and it was one that would stick throughout the child's life.

Once the dust had settled down upon the road and Claire's family returned to their own perspective homes, Aidan began to feel more and more at ease. The feeling that nothing good could last finally began to subside in the following months. He even began to believe that perhaps he had been all wrong after all. Maybe, just maybe, a body had only to traverse so many miles of rough, rocky, turbulent road in a lifetime. Maybe when his due had been paid by the miles in his mirror, a man would get to ease back into his seat and enjoy the drive. Maybe he thought, just maybe; but still there always remained a tiny nagging feeling that nothing good could last.

Claire too, was happier than she had ever been. In her mind, she had it all. She had her perfect man in Aidan, a perfect son, and lived in the perfect city. Unlike Aidan, however, she had no similar misgivings about being happy. In her mind, she had earned her happiness by always striving to do the right thing. She had waited to find the right sort of man instead of getting married right away when she turned sixteen or seventeen like many of her schoolmates had done. To her, happiness was an afterthought, an expected condition to those who lived well.

Whatever the case, the two came to love their lives together more with each passing day. Their son was only a symbol of their happiness for the world to see. Claire's favorite past time before had been her long walks and the birth of Dory had no effect on that. In fact, if anything, walking through the city with her baby leading the way in his stroller only made it all more wonderful. Now, not only could she awe at the architecture and admire the clouds passing over the lake or the shadows through the cityscape, but she could do all of that with a living symbol of her joy leading the way.

Claire walked through the city those days with a pride she had never known and a confidence she had never been able to express. Aidan was *her* husband, Dory was *her* beautiful baby that people stopped to 'oh' and 'ah' over, and Chicago was *her* city. Sometimes, during the day, she even began to take up shopping at Chicago's huge, fancy department stores. It wasn't to buy anything though, or even really to look at things that they couldn't afford and that she honestly didn't want anyways. It was so the women who did shop there could see her and admire her baby and deliver unto her the inevitable look of wishing they could trade all of their furs and diamonds to be her for just one day.

No. For Claire, this *was* her life and *nothing* would *ever* change. Even if it did change, it would only be to get better with perhaps another baby or five. There was no reason for it not to keep being great and getting better. She couldn't even imagine any such thing that could interfere with their happiness. To her, without the fear of loss or the knowledge of genuinely bad times in her life, it seemed unfathomable to think that it should be any other way. To her almost nothing could derail their happiness. To Claire, in her mind, it would take an act of God, or, or...another world war.

Chapter 38   Blown Away

It had only been a couple of weeks since little Dory had been born. The date was November 11, 1940 and the entire city was in motion to celebrate Armistice Day. Claire had been taking walks with her baby since her second day back home, and little Dory seemed to take to the cool fresh outside air.

By noon, the day had blossomed into one of the best in weeks. The sun shone brightly down into the city and the temperature climbed to sixty degrees. For Aidan it seemed almost an omen of the joy to come in his own life. The day, the walk, the time with his family, and the cheerful mood of the entire city on their day of celebration all came together neatly to paint a picture of things to come. That day, more than any other, if for only a few fleeting moments gave hope to him that the road ahead was truly beginning to rise to meet him.

Enjoying the day and each other, the couple pushed on and walked further than they normally might. Aidan loved to watch his beautiful wife beam with pride as people stopped to make faces at Dory. He turned them toward the famous Pier early that afternoon as it was certain to be abuzz with people and festivities. Sure, it was nearly three miles from their apartment, but it was a day that neither of them wanted to end, and despite the length of his tenure in Chicago, he had actually only been to the pier but once.

As they rounded yet another city block, the pier itself had finally come into view. But it was as close as they would get that day as the wind that began to blow nearly pulled the stroller from Claire's

174

hands. She almost never let Aidan push the stroller, but on this day, he had to take the reigns.

Turning back toward home to get away from what they had assumed to be lake wind, the couple was pursued by it. It began to seem that with each block, with each turn of the corner, the wind only grew in intensity. As they pushed on, the temperature too, began to plummet like a stone dropped in the deepest part of the lake itself.

As the couple rounded the last corner on their long walk home the stroller tore from Aidan's grip and rolled out into the busy Chicago street. Fortunately, by then, Claire had little Dory bundled inside of her own coat and wrapped in the light jacket Aidan had worn out that morning. It was the worst turn of a day's weather that either of them could ever remember.

By the time they reached their building that afternoon, the temperature had fallen to just slightly over twenty degrees and the wind howled outside. Walking in, the doorman held tightly to the door with both hands to keep it from slamming open in the wind and tearing off of its hinges. Across the street from them the thick metal sign that marked the corner market tore from the face of the brick building and smashed into a parked car nearby, then wafted high into the air again and disappeared altogether.

Aidan wondered if it wouldn't come careening down some blocks away and cut some poor unsuspecting man clean in half right where he stood. They were relieved to be back in their own home though, and Aidan rubbed his hands over his own arms as they climbed the stairs to their flat.

Inside, they were greeted by warmth as Claire un-wrapped little Dory. The baby himself gave the tiniest hint of a smile, apparently happy to be out of his cocoon and part of the world once again. But his enthusiasm would not last for long.

It was sometime around 7:00pm when it happened. Aidan sat nervously watching out the window of their apartment as the wind only grew with intensity as each hour ticked away. Claire stood in their small kitchenette, cleaning the last of their dishes from dinner. She startled and must have jumped a foot into the air when she heard the crash. She ran around the corner to find Aidan still sitting near the window covered in glass.

Everything in the apartment seemed to go into flight. The lamp flew off the end stand, papers soared into the air and Claire searched frantically for the baby. When she had left the room, Aidan had been sitting near the window holding him, but now, after the explosion, he was gone. Her heart sank as she concluded instantly that he must've been blown out the window. She screamed at Aidan who was picking large chunks of heavy glass off of him and trying to protect his face from flying debris.

"What?" He screamed back to her, but it was no use. The noise was as if a freight train were passing through their tiny apartment.

"Where is the baby?" She screamed again, holding on to a post, afraid to get any closer to the now open window for fear that she too would be sucked out.

Aidan pointed to the crib across the room near the door. Claire ran over and scooped Dory up into her arms, clutching him tightly. She was not about to let him blow away again, even if the first time had been an exaggeration in her own worried mind.

Aidan, having cleaned himself of the large, heavy shards of glass, opened the door into the hallway. They walked out, closing the door behind them securely. That night, they would huddle with dozens of other families in the crowded lobby of their building. Several windows had blown out during the course of the storm inviting the blizzard into a number of apartments. Countless more had simply retreated to the lobby to escape the shaking of the building and the fear of falling from great heights if it finally gave way and collapsed. Aidan couldn't figure the sense of them preferring to be at the bottom of the rubble pile should the structure give out than at the top, but he kept his thoughts on the matter to himself, realizing that such a statement would only further add to Claire's obvious distress.

What the couple had endured that night would come to be known as the great Armistice Day Blizzard of 1940. In Chicago, they would receive very little in the way of actual snow, but with winds as high as 70 miles per hour, thousands of windows succumbed to the pressure throughout the city, and when they finally relinquished, the entire City looked like a war zone with toppled trucks, garbage, tree limbs, and broken glass littering the streets.

Back home in Iowa, they would not be as fortunate. There, Claire would later learn, the blizzard had brought snow drifts over fifteen feet high. Her father had discovered twenty dead cattle, and reports were beginning to trickle in about dozens of motorists and hunters who had lost their lives by the surprise storm and its relentless intensity.

For Claire, the storm would be something to talk about and remember for the rest of her life. She would always say during future storms how it was never as bad as the Armistice Day storm when they had a blizzard come blowing right into their living room. But for Aidan it was something else. To him, it was but another omen that the road was ready to turn on him again. To Aidan, it was only a sign marking things to come and reminding him that no matter how far he had come from Melrose and his family and his past, that the curse was still very much upon him, watching, waiting, preparing to strike once more.

Chapter 39   Sunday Surprise

Much in the same way that the blizzard arrived shortly after their son, Aidan could not help but wonder what his first birthday might bring to their home. He never said anything to Claire about it, but the days following Dory's birthday brought him considerable anxiety. More and more as he aged, Aidan grew to believe in the ghosts of Melrose. More than ever, he believed in a curse that was seemingly linked to everything negative that befell him in his own life.

After a couple of weeks without disaster befalling them in any way, Aidan began to laugh at himself. He decided that he was not so far removed from his crazy grandfather after all, or that he was turning into MacGregor himself with his own funny beliefs in spirits and such.

Lately, he had been working more and more hours as the city, along with the nation itself seemed to be slowly and gradually climbing out of the effects of the depression. It seemed that even as his savings had been largely depleted, that his hours and wages had risen just enough for them to continue to live the lifestyle in their city flat that Claire had grown to love so much.

His feelings of impending doom had continued to plague him throughout the previous year, but Claire seemed to still be happy. There were tiny rifts in the conversation that had begun to form between them, largely as a result of Aidan keeping so much to his self lately. Generally speaking though, the road remained smooth and calm and both of them enjoyed at least a relative happiness doing the things that they each enjoyed. The winters were always the hardest of course, limiting the time that she had to spend outside and causing Aidan's routes to take much longer than normal, but they were getting by and life seemed, momentarily at least, just as it should be. Then, just as he least expected it, just as he let his guard down, it happened and everything changed in an instant.

Claire stood at the sink mixing some pancakes for a late breakfast. Aidan had decided to go out for a newspaper. It was a rare treat that they both enjoyed. He still could barely read following the accident, of course, but he liked to look at the thing nonetheless. He found that if he concentrated and cleared his mind, he could remember how to read some of the words slowly. He never let Claire know that he still couldn't read though, and picking up the newspaper and slowly thumbing through it became a habit that would follow him throughout the rest of his days.

The rest of the world did not take much notice of a man reading a newspaper. Still, to Aidan it quietly reaffirmed to the world around him that he could read as good as any of them, just in case anyone might be wondering.

Stepping out into the street, Aidan couldn't help but notice that for a Sunday in December the city seemed to be teaming with life. Everywhere he looked, people were moving about. Across the street, men stood in a huddle and appeared to be arguing back and forth. A pair of middle aged women ran by him best they could in their high heels, their faces filled with an expression that he could only equate with fear. As they passed, Aidan only looked oddly at their faces.

Turning away from them, he walked to the corner where the news-boy stood and gave the kid a couple of pennies. Raising the newspaper up, he slowed his breath and cleared his mind to slowly read the headlines. The paper read, *"Britain at War with Finland, Romania, Hungary."*

Aidan turned and walked back toward his building, continuing to look at the pictures on the front of the paper. It was odd to him.

There was no real surprise in the headline that people hadn't seen coming for weeks. It certainly wasn't news that would have so many people in Chicago running all about like chickens with their heads cut off. News of the wars in Europe and Asia made the headlines several times a week for the past couple of years and nobody seemed to care much in the streets of Chicago.

Just as Aidan reached his building, he saw Jerry, a man who drove out of the same warehouse as he did, come running up the street toward him.

"Aidan, did you hear the news?!?!" He said as he approached, slowing in his pace but with no apparent aim to stop altogether and chat.

"Yeah, I heard," he replied, still confused.

"It's the damnedest thing isn't it?" He said.

"Yeah, I guess so. But Britain has sort of been at war for a while now, right?" Aidan replied. Just then, Jerry stopped in his tracks. He had already blown past Aidan like a strong wind by at least ten feet when he stopped cold in his tracks and turned to face him.

"Oh my God," Jerry said, stepping back toward him. Aidan could tell then that Jerry had been crying.

"Are you crying? What's wrong? What's the matter with you?" Aidan pressed him. He didn't have many friends, even of the acquaintance variety like Jerry, and if one of them had something wrong, by God, he wanted to know about it.

"It's the God damned Japs," Jerry replied frantically, "they have attacked our base in Hawaii this morning. They murdered thousands of our boys today. We're going to war!"

"Oh my God," Aidan replied, feeling his entire body go sort of limp. He didn't exactly fall over, but the newspaper released from his hand and blew open. Neither he nor Jerry even seemed to notice as the pages blew, one at a time, down the sidewalk, and into the busy street.

Jerry was fast to be on his way headed for home. It seemed that everyone who was out that day hurried for home, only to turn round again and go into the street to talk things over with neighbors. That night in the city, angry mobs of men hell bent on revenge began to take shape. It was as if they'd thought they could form an old time posse right then and there to go deliver justice to the cowardly Japs for striking down so many American sailors asleep in their bunks. Everyone was angry and everyone wanted to do *something.*

Aidan and Claire had spent the next two days listening to the radio mostly. They, like so many Americans then, listened in horror and disbelief as the details of the attack were gruesomely relayed to them bit by bit and hour by hour. It was the sort of thing that none of them would ever forget where they had been when they heard it. It was the sort of thing that changed not only the rules, but the entire game itself. And to Aidan, it was the sort of thing that he knew had been barreling toward him like a piano dropped from the moon; falling faster and faster toward its inevitable target; him.

Despite her best of efforts, America was now at war and nothing would ever be the same again. Just as he had imagined, the road was about to get a whole lot rockier. All the same, just like hundreds of thousands of other Americans at that very moment in history, Aidan sat anxiously and nervously chomping at the bit to get started down it.

Chapter 40   Bitter Return

Claire held her baby and cried as the cab passed through Melrose. She tried not to, but in the end, she couldn't help herself. Albia was as close as they could get to her parent's farm south of Melrose by train. Instead of asking a relative to pick them up, Aidan had paid for a cab the rest of the way. Besides, he preferred surprise arrivals. Of course, everyone knew they were coming, but no one was for sure when.

Aidan and Claire didn't even know for absolute certain when they would be leaving Chicago. The Army seemed ill prepared to give out much information, mostly because they themselves didn't really know from one minute to the next.

Aidan had tried to fake his way through the rudimentary physical examination process. There really wasn't much to it after all. But, at some point during squats, he had cringed silently in pain and caught the attention of an Army doctor. He had believed that it would be the end of him to let on about his accident voluntarily and he was sort of right. The doctor quizzed him specifically and he let the cat slowly emerge from the bag about his lack of motor skills in his leg and hip, and the frequently recurring pain in his lower back as a result of the accident years before.

The doctor quickly pulled him from the ranks and began to draw up the paperwork to refuse him altogether, when through what amounted to idle conversation he revealed his experience as a truck driver. That, he would find, changed everything. The Army, for each of its trench digging, gun toting fighting men, he would discover, also required at least one other body driving trucks and running the warehouses that supplied them. With Aidan's experience behind the wheel of big rigs running difficult loads like swinging beef and even liquids at times, along with his ability to keep an old truck running using chewing gum and baling wire, he was the perfect candidate. The Army and his country would be able to use his services after all.

Claire was naturally less excited by the news. She had secretly prayed that he would be unable to serve, even though she knew that it would crush him to stay behind. She wanted vengeance wrought upon the Japanese as much as any other American did, of course. She had merely desired that it be wrought without the aid of her own husband and baby's father. In the end, she could hardly argue the point as talks were already being made about drafting all men of fighting age anyhow. No, it was better that he go on his own terms and doing that which he did best than to be stuck in some trench somewhere with a shovel and a rifle.

That she could live with. It would be her sacrifice to the war effort she had believed. It was only after enlisting that Aidan would inform her that her sacrifice would also mean leaving Chicago and return-ing to Melrose to live with her parents. That part of the deal was more than she had bargained for. How could she go from the excitement of the modern world back in time a hundred years to whence she had come? It seemed unconscionable to her to have to give up her husband and her home and the perfect quaint life that they had made together. It was more than any body should ever have to endure.

Aidan had dropped the bomb upon Claire, and then set them in motion while packing their belongings. It seemed that there was little more than time to get her back home and settled before he would be off to parts unknown for God knows how long.

"I will be home in six months," he promised her. "It will probably take them a month to get everybody rounded up, another to get them over there, a couple to beat the socks of em' and then we'll all be back home."

Even six months seemed to be forever to her then. Her life up to that point had been far from perfect, but it had been good enough for her. She had worked so hard to make everything in it just so, and now all of it was set to change. Seeing the town of Melrose, and then her parents was more than she could bear.

Walking up the path to her parent's home, she broke down and began openly weeping. Her mother rushed out the door upon hearing her. The old woman knelt, gathering her daughter's limp body up into the security of her own strong arms. Looking over her shoulder, she smiled empathetically at Aidan as he carried their bags from the departing cab.

It was odd to him to be back at the old MacGregor place. Especially since the touch of a woman had turned the entire place into something which it truly had never been before; a home. There were lacey curtains in all of the windows. The windows that he had always imagined to be made of faulted glass were so shiny and clean and glistened in the sun.

Aidan remembered back, when after his accident he had spent weeks staring out of those windows. He had developed an unusual skill of being able to judge what something was based on the size and coloration of the various blurs that passed by outside through the dirty haze. As it turned out though, they had only required a woman's touch and good scrubbing.

Only three days following their arrival in Melrose, Aidan would be on the train once again. This time he was headed back to Chicago to 'ship out' as it was called, to parts unknown. Before he left Melrose though, he and about a dozen other local residents were honored with a parade that ran right down Shamrock Street itself from atop the hill. The men, women and children all lined the street to see the local heroes off. They stood cheering and waving their flags as the men marched pass.

That was how he wanted to remember Melrose, he would later recall of the moment. For the moment, if only for that one moment even, he was not only just as one of them, but even above them a bit, held high above themselves as a hero of their own making. Any doubts that remained of his that the town might not have forgotten the details were washed away when they read his name through the bullhorn. The entire town cheered in unison "Hip! Hip! Hooray!" The answer resounded to the call of 'Aidan Keane.'

Even Claire herself seemed to be taken by the moment. As her husband passed, she held little Dory high in the air so the two could see one another. She knew that little Dory probably wouldn't remember. She still had wanted to say that he'd seen with his own two eyes as his father passed through town as a hero.

As Aidan walked slowly down the middle of the road though, he was struck by the oddest of feelings. Looking out at the waving flags and the crowds of people, he found himself searching the faces and the hair for Maizey in their midst. Try as he might to clear his head of it, his mind's eye flashed with a vision of her green eyes gazing upwards at him. In an instant, his entire body was awash with a warm sensation as he gazed back at the vision of those eyes with their beautiful tiny little droplets of chocolate in the tops, the left one twice as much as the right.

Odder still to him was saying good-bye. Aidan said all of his good-byes save one and it turned out to be the hardest by far. To his surprise, it wasn't even to Claire, but to his son. Claire, for her part even seemed resigned to the facts that had been thrust upon her. Secretly, Aidan wondered if she had mourned more for her loss of Chicago than for the potential permanent loss of her husband.

Aidan held his son close before he climbed into the cab. He kissed his soft head of red hair a couple of dozen times. He always loved the smell of his baby's hair. It was as divine a scent as he had ever inhaled. Strangely, in a way that he could not begin to describe, it even made him think of Maizey a little bit, of Dutchmen's Breeches flowers, and of simple things from his youth. After ten more minutes of holding his son close and smelling his hair and kissing his chubby cheeks he could hear the cab driver begin to grumble. Kissing his wife one last time, Aidan Keane turned away and climbed into the cab.

"Take me to the war," he said, giving a wave back to Claire and Dory and the rest of her family and extended family that had all gathered in the drive to see him off. Driving away from them all he looked back over his shoulder and furrowed his eyebrows at what he was feeling. He couldn't be certain, but in some strange sort of way that he couldn't even begin to explain, it was almost as if...he was somehow relieved.

Pulling into town, the cabby gave three short blasts with his horn to tell everyone that he had a VIP on board, and every able bodied soul outside over the age of three saw him off with cheers and big waves. It would seem that some things were even more important than your religion or where you came from and during that week at least, they were all only Americans. Aidan smiled back at each of them and waved to as many as he could before they cleared the edge of town.

It was a good day to be an American, he had thought. Hell, it was even a good day to be from Melrose, he added in his mind. Leaving the valley behind them, the cabby sped away, and Aidan headed off to war.

Chapter 41   Off To War

Aidan imagined that he would be swept from Chicago across the ocean where he would be driving a truck through enemy lines in a matter of weeks or even days. He had imagined wrong. Instead of heading toward the ocean, the Army sent him to camp Maxey near Paris, Texas.

Camp Maxey had been designated for infantry training and to his dismay, everyone in the Army including truck drivers had first to go through basic. The summer of 1942 in Paris, Texas was, in a word, hot. Some men would remember the details of daily life at basic training or the names of their fellow soldiers or their instructors. But mostly, Aidan only recollected that Paris, Texas was perhaps the hottest place on the face of the planet.

Still, there wasn't only the heat that created memorable experiences. The food was horrible as well. In fact, it would be the only time in his life that would cause him to reminisce fondly about MacGregor's mutton meat. It all began with the basic Army issue steel metal tray. The trays were impervious to food sticking to them only because they were never entirely washed from the prior usage and the entire tray was covered in about a quarter of an inch of grease.

Breakfast was by far the most dangerous part of the day because the runny, half cooked eggs had a tendency to want to slide off the greasy tray. The downside being, that spills were not only frowned upon by surrounding officers, but in basic training Aidan found that he couldn't eat nearly enough food to keep up with his body's increased demand.

Aside from that there was a lot of running and exercising involved at first. Due to his injuries, every step of the run sent shocking waves of electric pain coursing through his spine and throughout all of his limbs. While he could never have won a race with even the slowest of men, he always managed to keep up with the pack and not be singled out as one of those who constantly fell off pace.

Aidan learned quickly that the Army during war time was definitely not the place to be singled out. One such man who constantly fell off pace in the runs and marches was Fry. Fry was always being yelled at, and sometimes even beaten. All of it came to an abrupt halt the day he stood and struck an officer though. The MP's had him cuffed and were leading him away in minutes. Fry, feeling his oats however, thought that it would be funny to run from them. He got away too, for a few minutes.

Fry stood peaking around the corner of a barracks giggling in full view of Aidan and the rest of his unit, and all of them watched in horror as the MP walked up behind him, aimed his revolver, and pulled the trigger. Fry fell to the ground, twitched some, and died in a pool of blood.

Later, Aidan would deduce that what had transpired that day was a rather simple matter of war time logistics. The MP, being far more experienced in the ways of the Army had probably quite correctly concluded that he could chase Fry down, grapple with him, and then fill out about two dozen reports in triplicate and appear a half dozen days waiting as the trial is rescheduled OR he could shoot him dead on the spot for any number of legitimate reasons and simply fill out one form. It was a fitting introduction to the war time Army. These guys were not messing around and you had better not either.

Basic was followed by an abbreviated transportation course for experienced drivers on how to do everything the Army way. Then it was on to New York where after several weeks of waiting, Aidan would finally board a ship bound for parts unknown. The rumors aboard the vessel were that they were going to land somewhere in Portugal and be part of a major push into the heartland of Europe.

As Aidan would soon learn, however, the rumors you heard while in the Army were almost always, and with damned few exceptions, dead wrong. Instead, he would join thousands of other men in a holding base in the south of England. There, Aidan and tens of thousands of other American G.I.s would hunker down against the harsh British weather and do what they would learn to best in the Army...wait.

For men supposed to be off fighting a war, you'd have hardly known it. In fact, if it weren't for the constant air raids and black outs, you wouldn't have really known it at all where they were stationed in the English countryside. Mostly, they were bored out of their minds more than anything. Many of the men even made up stories in their letters home rather than admit that they were just sitting around or spending all of their time over the past eighteen months chasing the man starved local women.

Aidan, though, never sent any lies back home in his letters to Claire. Fact was that they seldom sent any letters back and forth at all. It was as if the distance and separation only caused each of them to realize how little they actually depended upon one another emotionally. Aidan did love her and he loved being with her. They always had a good time together too. But, still he wondered, what did it mean that he didn't seem to miss her that much? What could it mean? In fact, the only thing that really did bother him was that he wasn't all that bothered by it.

Chapter 42   Spoils of War

After the invasion had taken place, Aidan finally landed on the continent along with the truck that he had been assigned in England. For almost a year, he had performed daily maintenance and cleaning on his truck as it sat in a hangar in Whales. Finally, he and his truck would get some action.

With more experience than most of the men driving in his newly formed division, Aidan got the cream of the crop in the form of a huge 5-ton International cargo hauler. It was the truck that he would be with until the end of the war, or until the end of *his* war at least.

The first mission of his division was supply, but the secondary mission was return. The secret order was that no truck was to return to the storage depot empty handed. There were hundreds of officers back there thirsty for goodies to send home to prove that they had been in the war and it was up to the drivers to keep them supplied with a steady flow of German goods.

Much of what they brought back during the European theatre was traded for hard to get items to front line troops. Things like a six pack of American beer, or an extra carton of cigarettes could fetch you a Nazi rifle or the like from the boys who saw the front line action. But as the Germans were pushed further back into their Alamo in Berlin and the supply convoys flowed into the homeland, virtually everything German became up for grabs.

It was expected that no truck return without some sort of German booty, and the result was the almost systematic pillaging of the German countryside by American troops. Aidan would take his own share of the spoils as did the rest, but one place in specific would always remain in his memory.

Aidan had just been offloaded and was eager to get back to make one more load for the day. There was a rumor circulating that with the trains full up and running in France that they were going to transfer all of the colored drivers from the Red Ball Express Road operation forward, and reassign all of the white drivers. The mid level officers recognized that if that happened, their spoils of war operation would grind to an abrupt halt because no one was going to have a bunch of black drivers out looting. It just didn't reflect well upon the nation, it was thought. Anyhow, as a result, they were calling on the white forward drivers to double their tonnage to save their own routes and all of their asses.

Aidan stopped outside the small rural village of Leitersweiler, just south and west of Freisen. It was as safe an area as you could find inside the German borders, but you still had to go at least an uncomfortable distance off of the main road to find unoccupied homes that hadn't been looted yet. The countryside around Leitersweiler had been hastily and almost completely abandoned though and there was little threat from remaining snipers, even for the bigger 5-ton trucks like Aidan's.

Looking out across the slow rolling terrain that surrounded him, Aidan was reminded of home. The hills were larger and sprawled over miles of earth, but the fields and wooded lots were the closest thing to home that he had seen in all of Europe. Pulling alongside the road he wondered what the weather was like back home just then, and if the sun had shone just as brightly upon Melrose as it was now shining on him.

Walking up the rocky lane toward the farmhouse, he gripped his pistol and checked it once for good measure. Half way up the lane, he paused to investigate the click, click, clicking noise coming from his left boot. A piece of the sharp driveway shale had cut into the side of his boot sole. "God damned shale," he said quietly to himself, pulling the shard out of his boot and tossing it into the grass so that it couldn't re-offend upon the next poor unsuspecting soul.

Approaching the farmhouse, he stopped momentarily and took it in. It would definitely be a good one if someone else hadn't gotten to it yet. It was a huge, sprawling two story number, probably more than two hundred years old. The first floor was done in German white-washed stucco over stone, topped with a second floor all in exposed hardwoods. The second floor had a wrap around porch on the entire house, causing the whole of it to appear somewhat top heavy, as if a strong wind could topple the thing.

The entire front of the house was surrounded by a neatly kept garden of flowers and herbs and a handful of vegetables. The garden itself was surrounded by a white picket fence, which, for whatever reason, was also the only unkempt thing on the property, badly in need of a fresh coat of whitewash. Aidan raised his weapon near his head as he entered through the picket gate and approached the house.

Walking inside, Aidan hollered to see if anyone was inside, but there came no reply. Either it was unoccupied, or someone was going to wait and surprise him. He had been in dozens of homes in the countryside and he felt as if this one was clear. If the war had taught him anything, it had been to trust in his own instincts. He holstered his weapon, but left it unbuttoned just in case.

On more than one occasion, his gut feelings had kept him alive. Like the time the entire convoy had been strafed by German fighter planes. They had lost two dozen drivers that day. Aidan had veered off at the last minute and taken a different route. There was just something that he hadn't liked about the route they had proposed to take that day. Looking back, he could only say that he didn't like the feel of that particular stretch of road.

Looking through the house, it was as if he had hit the mother land's mother lode. There was ancient silverware lining the walls all around him and steins and figurines and every imaginable sort of antiquity, and on almost every wall in every room, there was even an oil painting or two. Those would definitely be going along with him. There was a certain high ranking officer back at HQ who was paying premiums for old oil paintings and other antiquities.

Aidan threw out three duffels on to the floor of the main room and unrolled them to begin to fill up on loot. Then he saw them. There, right in front of his face at eye level, upon a three hundred year old hand-carved bureau, were the faces of the residents staring back at him. Aidan rose slowly to his feet as he looked at the photos. He was frozen for a second in a state of confusion. He could feel his heart sink into the pits of his stomach and a hint of the flavor of bile filled his mouth as his knees quivered beneath him.

Reaching out, he picked up the largest of the frames and held it in front of him staring at it. It was her. It wasn't really her, of course, but it *was* her. Maizey stared back at him from the photo. It was her, exactly the way that he remembered her, the flow and length of hair with the hundreds of light colored natural curls in it; the smile that warmed his heart and moved his soul. Except for the missing drops of chocolate in the eyes that were staring back at him, it *was* her. Then, like a bomb, it hit him. He nearly went limp as his entire body was awash with a state of utter loneliness.

"My God," he said staring at the photo. "My God," he whispered again. As he spoke, tears streamed down his cheeks, dripping on to the dark, smooth, worn hardwood floor at his feet.

It was there in a German farmhouse halfway around the globe that he realized that he wasn't over her; he would never be over her. She was the living breathing link to everyone he had lost in his life and everything that he had held dear from his past. He wished that she could be with him just then, there in that farmhouse. They could take over caring for the garden, and he could tend to the crops in the field. Together, they could live right there and be completely happy and have a dozen children. But alas, she wasn't there. She never would be. He could only stand looking at a face just like hers, weeping to the screaming lonely sound of the silence in the house.

Aidan knelt and slowly rolled up his duffels and left the house exactly as he had found it. On the front door he marked it as a safe house for a high ranking officer whose name did not exist. Many of the officers had staff following the frontline action assigned to mark out property to be left untouched by American GI's, and Aidan was familiar with their style of marking the doors. With the mark of a high enough rank, Patton himself would not molest the home again.

He returned to base empty handed that day. It was the last home or business that he would enter. It was too personal, too wrong he felt, to walk into places that didn't belong to you and take things from people who may not have even been the perpetrators behind the Nazis and their atrocities. Besides, any one of the homes could belong to another girl just like her. He would have no part of it any more.

His commanding officer was not quite as impressed with his new-found morals however, and after half a dozen loads were returned empty handed, he was reassigned to driving ambulances. It was the worst duty that a white driver could pull short of hauling ordinance. But since the Luftwaffe had been all but wiped out anyways, hauling ammunition and ordinance or even fuel wasn't the death sentence that it had once been. Now, as the final push to Berlin raced forward, it was the ambulances that were the worst.

There would be few nights for the rest of his days that he would not awaken at some point, often in a sweat, to the sound of the screams and moans of the wounded soldiers. Worst of all was the smell of death that he carried with him everywhere. If he picked up a dozen injured men on a trip, it was not uncommon to find a third or better of them dead by the time he got to the hospital. It would fall upon him, the driver, to unload them at the morgue and then hurriedly clean the back of the truck out as best he could without the proper supplies or hot water. Of course, you never got it all, and the stench only became more unbearable as the days wore on.

The assignment lasted just long enough to ruin his sleep for the rest of his life before the bulk of the war in Europe would finally be over. With the war's end also came the full extent of Army bureaucracy with thousands of pencil pushers filling every available building and intruding upon nearly every aspect of their daily life. Once again, like so many times before in Army life, boredom set in as thousands simply laid down their arms, parked their trucks and waited. There would still be hundreds of injuries and casualties of course, but they were fewer and farther between and ambulance drivers waited their turn on duty, sometimes for three or four days before receiving an assignment.

For Aidan, it was the end of the war. He had never really even carried his rifle, and had never fired even his pistol in anger. There was the time when he found a German couple hiding in a closet, but he had only pointed the weapon at them momentarily. There had, however, been shots fired at him a dozen times and potential danger loomed large on every road, but what would haunt him the most were the bodies and the screaming, dying soldiers, along with a picture he had found in a farmhouse in Germany. Those things, he would never speak of again, and he would never fully get over them either.

It was only days after his son's fifth birthday in October of 1945. He received two things that day at mail call; his orders to return to the states and a rare letter from home.

Chapter 43   The Long Road Home

Aidan remembered thinking that he should have been more upset by
what the letter had said. He should have been sad and lost and
hopeless, but he wasn't any of those things. What he felt instead was
an odd sort of relief. Claire had written to say that she had left Dory
with her parents to take a job, of all places, in Chicago. She said that
they were paying a lot of money for women to work there nowa-
days, and she could barely afford not to go. She added that she was
using the money that he had sent home and she had saved, but that
Dory, as well as his small collection of German firearms, would be
waiting for him in Melrose. She ended succinctly with the words,
"I'm not coming home. Please don't look for me."

There it was. He imagined what poor little Dory must be going
through and his heart ached for him, but he also reckoned that his
grandparents had been playing the leading role in his absence
anyway. Claire had seemed the perfect mother, but he always
suspected that she only loved the attention that having a baby drew
for her. At some point, as the cuteness of the baby wore off, the
toddler, and then little boy, began more and more to appear only as
baggage in her mind.

Aidan had a pilot friend read the letter to him only once and then he
sat quietly for a few moments. Afterwards, he turned and threw it
into the waste can. His friend, Captain Ronald Morgan from Southern Illinois sat staring at him, waiting for him to explode into fury
or cry or show some form of emotion, but the expected outburst
would never materialize. Ronald would place his hand on Aidan's

shoulder, but Aidan would only hand him his orders and ask him to read them as well. Aidan had claimed that he had vision problems but Morgy, as he was called by his friends, suspected that he couldn't read. To his credit though, he never uttered a word of it to Aidan or anyone else.

Fraternization between enlisted men and officers was strictly pro-hibited of course, but the war was nearly over and all of them were eager to return to a sense of normalcy. Besides, with Morgy flying supply planes and Aidan driving supplies and bodies, they had shared the same stale coffee and assignment ready rooms for hours and even days at a time on countless occasions over the past several months. Now, both of them would be going home soon as well, so there was little in either of their minds tying them down to what they considered to be stupid Army regulations.

Aidan's orders called for him to report via transport, then ship, to New York to begin out processing in thirty days. It was finally over. He might get hung up in out processing somewhere for another month or two after that though, because this still was the Army where everything took a hundred times longer than it should.

Then Morgy hit him with it. He would be flying a direct transport home in a couple of days. He had just drawn the assignment. Aidan could hitch a ride with him and be in the states in a matter of hours instead of being stuck on a crowded ship for several weeks. Aidan remembered the cramped conditions and the smell of hundreds of men throwing up for weeks as they had inched their way across the Atlantic in a steam ship that probably had carried pilgrims across three hundred years earlier. The trials and tribulations of the journey had been a large part of his reasoning, and that of many young men who had arrived earlier in the war, for passing on a furlough back home or anywhere else. It just wasn't worth it.

Aidan had never flown before, but he had spent hours waiting at the various advancing supply depots watching the huge planes come and go. The fighter planes were too fast and quite honestly, scared the hell out of him to even watch. But the big transport planes seemed to just float through the air. Morgy also sweetened the deal by adding that they were headed for an air base in South Carolina and that Aidan could then take his own sweet time over the next several weeks slowly bumming his way up the Atlantic coast, admiring the girls and drinking toddies. He jumped at the chance.

The airplane was a Curtiss Wright C-46 Cargo Plane, and Morgy and friends were flying the thing home to use for a training model. The Army had finally reached the point where more pilots could be trained on the actual planes that they would use overseas now that the action was dying down and they were eager to get a few back home. The airplane was a huge, fat, stout, beast of a machine. To Aidan it resembled an elongated football and upon closer inspection walking up to the thing, he wondered in awe at how something so huge could be made to fly.

Aidan sat with a handful of other men on the half dozen fold down seats that lined the walls behind the pilots. It was everything that he could do not to show his nervousness for the other three men on board to see. He kept on reassuring himself as the plane shook while the engines fired up. He tried to keep from gasping too conspicuously as the plane shimmied and accelerated down the runway. But as the huge plane caught the air and just as he thought everything would be alright, it banked hard left on a turn and simultaneously passed long ways into the heavy wind. The entire airplane dropped what seemed like twenty feet and then snapped back upwards into the sky. Aidan let loose a curse and the other men smiled nervously back at him, clutching on to their seat bottoms for dear life.

In the end though, the three terrifying take-offs and landings weren't even the worst of it really. The worst of it turned out to be the bone chilling, freezing cold in the high elevations for countless hours on the cold unforgiving hard metal seat. It would serve as a stark reminder for him though, that nothing about the Army, or the war effort, had been built for comfort. It was all about getting the men and materials where they had needed to be, and getting them there alive, even if only barely.

During the worst of it when the cold set deep into his aching joints and every bone in his body seemed to scream out in pain, and when the airplane had been seemingly ready to shake apart in the clouds of a rising storm over the ocean; while all of that was going on and he was certain that he was going to die, he remembered thinking of little Dory back home; the smell of his hair and how soft he felt holding him close. But also he thought again of Maizey. She was always there, popping into his thoughts when he needed her most or wanted to think of her the least. Hers was the one face besides Dory's that always flashed through his mind's eye. More than any of the rest of the ghosts who would come to call upon him, it was always Maizey. Always. Two tiny droplets of chocolate, he thought to himself, the left one twice as much as the right, and the airplane banked once more for it's final descent into South Carolina.

Walking off of the base, Aidan was thankful to have survived the trip. In fact, it would be the last time his feet would ever leave the ground to fly again. He'd take the slow rolling sea sickness, he decided, any day over the hell ride he had just endured. Even the searing Carolina heat would take the better part of a day to work the aching, burning cold out of his bones and joints.

There in South Carolina, hundreds of miles from anywhere Aidan had ever called home, he stopped in the road and mused at the familiarity of his situation. He stood along the edge of the road winding back toward the ocean and placed a foot on the railroad tracks where they crossed the road heading to points unknown back west. He could smell the warm, salty ocean air blowing softly across his face in one hand and the familiar scent of fresh creosote and oiled gravel upon the other.

Smiling, he turned and began to walk down the tracks, balancing himself as he went at first and then just walking, taking in the air and sights and scents around him. The Army, he figured, would not miss just one GI. He would be right, of course, and would receive his official discharge papers almost a year later via the U.S. Mail. He would wonder if the elapsed time would have been equivalent to how many months he would have had to have mill about in New York or some other base, and it reassured him once again in the ability of his own gut to choose the best road to travel in life.

Chapter 44   The Railroad

Aidan would spend a couple of days just walking along the rails, enjoying being back in the States. The tiny towns that lined the tracks were all still jubilant from the Allied victory in Europe and welcomed the sight of any passing body that happened to be in uniform. Although his pockets were stuffed with cash, he was unable to use any as the rural diners not too close to the major military bases refused to accept payment from returning GIs.

Aidan figured that the folks he encountered were reminded of other local boys who had yet to return or who would never be coming home at all. Through their kindness to him, he reckoned, they could hope that someone, somewhere, would be doing the same for their own local heroes. Also, it was a way for them to pay tribute to their fallen.

Running into the mainline near Knoxville, he managed to hitch on an empty freight car and ride it northward through Louisville and into Indianapolis. There he switched cars to head into Chicago. Unlike the recent years when railroad cops chased and beat freeloading hijackers, many of them even stopped to talk to the man in uniform or simply pretended not to see him altogether.

In Chicago, Aidan stopped to rest in the rail yards. Lying under a nearby shade tree eating an apple, he toyed with the idea of looking for his wife while he was in town, but in the end he decided it best to leave her wherever, and with whomever, she might be. He was preparing to get up and find the train home when the railroad foreman ambled out of the office shack. The man stopped and eyed him from afar, then began walking toward him.

"You just back stateside, fella?" The large man waddled slowly toward him, his unbuttoned, unseasonably warm flannel shirt, blowing in the light wind behind him as he neared.

"Yes, sir. Just back in from beautiful sun shiny Germany," Aidan said, smiling broadly. He had yet to figure from what angle the large man approached him, and thought it best to greet him with a smile and a bit of charm.

"Where you headed to? Or do you aim to live right here in my rail yard," he asked, but returned the smile so that Aidan could see he was only pretending to be upset by his presence in friendly jest.

"Iowa eventually, Sir," Aidan replied, standing up to shake his hand as the large, round man was nearly atop him by then. "But I could stay here for a night or two if you need the company and don't mind sharing your apples from that there tree."

The large man laughed, "Nope," he replied. "You take as many apples as you want. It ain't my tree. George Stevens is the name," he said, shaking Aidan's hand. "And if you aren't in any hurry, I could actually use a hand. That is, if you're looking for a job right yet."

"Aidan Keane," he said, shaking the man's hand and studying his eyes to see if he was still joshing him or not.

Aidan thought about the offer. There were two things that had always interested him as a child, the road and the railroad tracks, and both of them had led out of Melrose. He had spent most of the last decade behind the wheel of a truck and he could have kept right on doing it too, but driving in Europe had changed him somehow. He didn't get as much joy out of it as he once had. Whereas, once it seemed like a way out of somewhere, going to somewhere else, it now only seemed like he had been driving around in big circles, heading nowhere.

"I'll take the job," he said.

"Fine," Stevens replied. "Come with me and we'll get you signed up. You'd be amazed at how hard it has become to find decent help while the damned war was going on."

Aidan picked up the duffel bag containing most all of his remaining worldly belongings and followed Stevens back across the rail yard. Stevens, as it turned out, had received his bad limp during the Normandy invasion. He had been part of a landing team slated to hit Omaha beach. They had lost their bearing however and hit a stretch of beach alone. The entire team was killed or injured before a single man left the transport. Stevens had been one of the lucky few who was hit early and covered by the bodies of his brothers as they absorbed countless rounds of fire.

"I guess that we all lose our bearing sometimes," Stevens had said after recounting the story of how he came to have his limp, "don't we?"

"Yes, sir, Mr. Stevens," Aidan replied. "Yes, we certainly do."

"Well, Aidan," he said with a smile, returning from his far away daze he had been in while he recounted his story. "Thank God for the railroad though. It will get us both back on track. You can't lose your bearing if you stick to the rail," he said, adding, "and every mile of track ahead is as smooth as the last."

Aidan looked at him and raised an eyebrow, but Stevens only smiled back at him, handing him some papers to sign. He couldn't have known how Aidan had always looked ahead at the road and at life, comparing the two in his mind. He couldn't have known either what the road or the rails had meant to him personally, but in that instant, hearing those words, he did know that he was in the right place at the right time and doing the right thing for himself. He was due for smooth tracks, for no worries about the constantly changing roads ahead. Aidan signed the papers where he was told, and followed Stevens back out across the rail yard toward his future.

Chapter 45   The Long, Smooth Road

Aidan knew there was no sense in trying to really find Maizey. It was foolish to think even for a second that she would be waiting for him after all of those years. Waiting, hell, she probably wouldn't even remember him. But still, he always held the memory of her and their summer together dearest to his heart of hearts. While he would never again remarry, he would have many lovers. Often, these were during the winter months only to find that in his mind he could not help but compare them to his memory of her. None of them would ever last much into spring and the summer would always be hers. Always.

His job that began in the rail yards of Chicago would last him the rest of his working life. Only months after being hired on that day, Aidan would bid on, and receive a position as a track laborer that would enable him to live back in southern Iowa and be closer to Dory. The transient life of a railroad worker though never really lent itself to becoming a full-time parent. As a result, Dory would split his time between his grandparents outside of Melrose and the small house that Aidan had purchased near the station in Chariton, some fifteen odd miles to the north and west.

Dory never seemed to fully recover from being left by his parents though. Even as his father was in his life half the time and his mother visited him several times a year with her new husband from Chicago. He was always rather child-like, Aidan had thought, even as he grew older. Dory would grow into a man and get a job as was expected of men, and people generally liked him too. But still, there was a part of him that remained a very small boy inside and it always troubled Aidan. It was as if no matter what he had done for him, and he tried to give him the world, that there remained a part of his son that no one could reach, distant and aloof and immature.

Aidan had held a grand total of three jobs in his entire life, including working for MacGregor. Dory would go through as many in one summer and spend the winter that followed loafing about the house while Aidan worked on the railroad. For his part, in a way, Aidan began to withdraw from his son. The aging man would begin to spend more and more of his time in Chariton or Melrose sitting at the tavern. In the end it seemed, he had only returned home from the war to become one of the aging petrified mummies quietly filling a bar stool every night.

When Aidan had a chance to, he hunted with friends who had survived the old days. As the nineteen sixties progressed and the deer began to slowly return to Iowa, he even formed a group of his own to hunt them with. There was old man Harris, who kept himself alive it seemed, only by constantly nipping bourbon from his silver flask. And Morgy, the pilot from Illinois would fly his single engine plane over every year from his factory job in Moline and join them. There were even a handful of old Irish Catholic ruffians from Melrose who Aidan had attended school with years before who would join them on their hunt and the drunken festivities that would follow each evening.

They were good times, to be certain, and he was among friends, but still, he felt alone in the world, and he would never mention Dory. The other men would always ask after the young man of course, but he preferred not to speak of him and replied to all queries in quick, terse, one word answers.

Aidan, for all of his stubborn pride, was ashamed. But he wasn't ashamed of his son like everyone, including Dory himself, believed to be the case. Rather, he was ashamed of himself for having ruined him. He had been too self absorbed through it all. He had been too concerned about his own thoughts and feelings and wants and needs to ever put his son first, he believed. And anything that had become of him, whatever the boy had grown to become, was Aidan's doing and his alone.

As his son's failures in life mounted, so too did the burden upon the aging man's shoulders that he had failed him and been his ruin. It was the curse of Devils of the Dump, he believed. It was real and it was alive, working through him to deliver the family heirloom of misery on to the next generation of tortured souls. In the end, he could barely stand to look his own son in the eyes.

Once, as Aidan sat in a Chariton bar drinking, Dory walked in. He stood proudly in front of his father holding a huge catfish he had caught that morning. It was one of the few things the two had shared in this world; their love of fishing. Aidan smiled politely, but in his shame, he quickly looked away, ignoring his son as the other men commented on the fish.

In 1967, when Dory was caught trying to rob a local store, Aidan paid his fines, reimbursed the store owner, and begged the local magistrate, himself a war veteran, for lenience. When he was arrested again in 1969 on drug charges, Aidan bailed him out of jail and paid for an expensive attorney to come down from Des Moines and help him beat the charge. And when Dory had been watching the house in 1972 while Aidan was working out on a train derailment and his entire collection of guns, including his German rifles from the war came up missing, he shoved the chief of police out his front door for suggesting that Dory himself probably had something to do with it.

In the end, everyone in the world could see what was going on except for the man closest to it all. Aidan trudged through each day carrying the heavy load upon his weary shoulders that he had caused it all. He blamed himself for everything that his son endured and wrestled with the guilt each morning of wondering where he was when his bed was empty. A jail cell? A drug house? Dead somewhere? God only knew, but wherever it was, it was due entirely to Aidan's negligence and the curse he had passed through his blood to the boy.

The boy of course, wasn't a boy at all any more. He was a grown man in his early thirties. But still, to Aidan he would always be the infant son he had left behind in Melrose. At times when he thought about casting him out, the smell of his infant hair would still fill his nostrils as if it were only yesterday when he said good-bye to go off to war.

He should have stayed, he'd thought to himself. He should have made the boy's mother come home. He should have done so many things differently, but he hadn't and now Dory was left to pay for each of Aidan's own selfish sins. It was almost more than he could bear. But still, during the worst of it all, when the midnight phone call came or the police showed up at his doorstep again, he would always think of Maizey. She would always be there comforting him with her tiny drops of soothing chocolate in her eyes, smiling up at him. Always.

Chapter 46   Ohio

Maizey had spent the majority of her entire first year back in Ohio crying herself to sleep at night. It was as if a piece of her very soul had been ripped from her body. There is something about a woman's first love, she believed, that just stuck in her craw for the rest of her days, no matter how the thing may have ended. But the worst kind of first love was what she had endured; the sort that ends abruptly, killed by circumstances beyond your own control.

No matter how strong the bond of love between two people, she had later thought, you could break it. It may be difficult to endure, watching it die, but it could be done and a body could move forward. A first love that is ripped apart though, one that dies a speedy and unnatural death like theirs had, well, that just sort of haunts you until the day that you die. It tears a part of your heart and soul out of your chest and you never quite get it back. It is always there like a wound that never heals and given the right time of year, the scent of fresh hay, or the sight of that certain sort of flower, it all comes rushing back and the pain is as fresh as the morning dew on a sultry summer day.

It was silly of her to ponder upon such things from so long ago and from a time when she was only a child herself, but a girl's heart is always only that, a girl's heart, whether she be sixteen or sixty, and the hundred secret tears and wounds that have been placed upon it are never fully healed.

Still, she had moved forward in her life and at twenty years of age, she fell in love. With all of the men that she had dated, she had always sort of held them into the light and turned them to and fro in her mind, comparing them against her own glorified memory of Aidan. William was not as fun, nor as funny as Aidan. Nor was he as passionate. But he was a very handsome man with a good job, a bright future, and more than all of that, he loved her.

In the end she decided to put away her own childish things and soothe her wounded heart by basking in the rejuvenating warmth of a man who truly loved her and would never leave her side. To his credit, as promised, William never did leave her side until the day that he died. The two were never able to have any children, but they still had managed to find happiness and comfort and joy in one another.

On their fortieth wedding anniversary the couple was given a surprise party by their relatives, friends, and William's co-workers. Almost a hundred people showed up too. Maizey was never quite as happy to be among so many friends as she had been on that day. Her younger brother, always the sneak, had even managed to find a bunch of ancient pictures of the couple and made a collage on poster boards. Maizey remembered him needing to get into the house while they were out of town. He had said that he needed to borrow her carpet steamer after a nasty spill, but then she knew what he had really been up to.

Admiring the pictures, Maizey dropped her coffee right where she stood. There, amongst all the others of her and her husband was the one surviving picture that she had from that first summer. Aidan stood tall and proud smiling at the camera with his foot on the running board of someone's car in Melrose as if it were his very own. She stood beside him leaning in with her hands resting on his chest. She hadn't seen that picture in years. It still bore the stains on it from a thousand tears.

Fortunately, her spilled coffee had become the attention grabber and no one else would notice the one picture in a crowd of a hundred, not even her own husband. But she had, and she could scarcely believe how the emotions and feelings and sights and sounds and smells from so long ago could just come flooding back to the surface like that.

Smiling and wiping away the tears that so many believed were tears of joy about the moment and the day and the celebration, Maizey slowly regained control and pushed her scarred heart deep back into the corner of her chest where she had stored it all of those years. Then she turned to her husband of forty years, smiled, kissed him, and thanked him for loving her and giving her the best years of his life and her own.

Chapter 47   1977

Aidan was awakened early that morning to the sound of dying men screaming in the back of his ambulance. His nostrils were filled with the smell of death that hung heavy in the room. He sprung out of bed and went quickly to open the window, allowing the brisk fresh air of the early autumn morning to rush in across his face.

Walking down the stairs to start his coffee and wash away the whiskey from the night before, he looked in Doran's bedroom. It was empty again. His heart sank as it had done a thousand times before as he continued on down into the kitchen. On the table there was a note stating simply, "I'm sorry."

Aidan turned around and looked at the jar atop the fridge where he kept his cash. It was gone. Then he walked out into the living room and stared in disbelief at his gun case where his shotgun and hunting rifle were kept. The lock had been hastily busted open sparing the etched glass front at least, thank God, but all of his guns were missing. He felt the urge to be sick, but he only shuffled back out to the kitchen and started his coffee.

Sitting there at his kitchen table he finally came to terms with what he would have to do. When Dory finally returned home, he surmised, it would be his last return. He would have his things packed and waiting for him. His fault or not, the boy had just turned thirty-seven years old and enough was more than enough. He could either make it or die the death of a junky, starving under a bridge somewhere.

Two days passed and then three. Aidan didn't even go the bar during that stretch as he didn't want to give Dory the chance to sneak in and steal a bite to eat only to leave again before he could return home. Aidan sat up at the kitchen table and waited.

On the third day, one of Dory's last childhood friends stopped at the house. Aidan told him what had happened and ended with, "When you see him, tell him that he won't be welcome here any more."

Dory's friend went out to the old MacGregor family farm where he often held up in the barn after a long binge to deliver the message. He had thought that it was best, as this time, the old man looked as though he might kill him given half the chance to do so. Walking into the barn, his friend found him. Dory had shot up with the last of the drugs he had bought with his father's money, placed the end of the shotgun into his mouth, and pulled the trigger. When his friend had found him, he was stiff as a board. The sheriff even had to use a chunk of iron to pry the gun out of his hands.

The men who hunted with Aidan came from all over and stayed with him for weeks. Morgy, himself a widower, even took an early retirement and stayed on with him for several months before returning to Illinois. They had almost all thought that it would be the straw that would break him. For weeks, no one would leave him alone, and it would be months before they would let him have a gun.

In the end though, Aidan had endured so much pain and misery in his life that he had almost come to expect it, no, rely upon it. Losing his son was the worst sort of pain he had ever known, but still, it was only pain. It was only another stretch of painful, shale covered road that was his to endure. A fitting end, he believed, to the life he had lived, and the curse that had followed him through the ages.

For Dory at least, he thought, the curse was over. The pain had stopped at least. He would not live to know the heartache of losing the people that he cared most about in this world. For that one thing, and that thing alone, Aidan was grateful. For everything else though, he had little left of himself to care about.

Shortly after *the accident*, as he would come to call it in his own mind, he officially took his own retirement. Work, driving, the railroad; it had all been his way of escaping the pain in his life. But for the first time in his life, he couldn't even bring himself to try to escape. Once again, the ghosts, plus one more, came a calling. Once again, he would greet them completely alone.

For three years, each day became like the last. It would begin with an old man sitting at the bar drinking beer and a whiskey or two. He had finally become one of them; the lifeless, aging, gray-skinned, hopeless forms who haunt the bars and taverns during the daylight hours. They come not to socialize or mingle, but to sit quietly, staring in the mirror across the bar into the depths of their own souls and drink away the ghosts that haunt them.

Chapter 48   Morgy's Revenge

Shortly after Morgy had lost his wife, it had been Aidan who came and dragged him off to the Canadian Boundary waters on a fishing trip. It had been the last thing that he had desired to do at that point in time, but it had turned out to be the best thing that he could have done. The clear skies and clean waters had touched his soul and drew him closer to finding an inner peace with the events and the world as a whole.

Morgy had tried to return the favor ever since Dory had died, but Aidan would have nothing of it. They used to joke that Aidan would find him a woman only long enough to keep his feet warm for the winter and then shed himself of her each spring as the weather improved. But since Dory had died, he hadn't even bothered with them any more. Truth was, it had been the winters spent with women, staying out of the bars and actually eating home cooked food that had kept him going as long as he had. By all accounts, Aidan's health was fading quickly, so Morgy knew that this would probably be his last attempt to save his old friend.

The door of the Sportsman's Bar on Chariton's Southside swung open and the man stepped in, stopping for a moment while his eyes slowly adjusted to the darkness. The old man who owned the bar turned his attention away from the afternoon baseball game and walked down to greet the stranger.

"What can I get for you?" the bar owner asked politely, smiling a warm greeting to the stranger. They didn't get many strangers in the bar any more since the evening crowd had become rougher and less tolerant of outsiders in recent years, and God only knew that he could use the business.

"I'd like an Old Milwaukee," Morgy replied, returning the smile and setting a twenty on the bar. "And get one for the old Irish drunk at the end of the bar."

"You mean Aidan?" the bar owner asked.

"That would be he," Morgy replied.

At that, Aidan turned and looked down the bar. His face lit into a smile as he recognized his old war buddy through the smoky haze. "Hey! What the hell are you doing here?" Aidan asked.

"I've heard you Southern Iowa boys was an unfriendly lot," he replied, "but I didn't figure you would have a beef with a fella just stopping in for beer."

The other drunks, sensing the familiarity between the two, turned back away and watched the game. Aidan got up and walked down the bar. The two shook hands and grabbed each other's shoulders, stopping just short of hugging.

Aidan pulled up a stool beside him at the bar and the bar owner placed the beers in front of them. New faces meant new stories and more gossip, so the bar owner, while turning his attention back toward the game, stayed within ear shot of the two men.

"What brings you?" Aidan inquired, taking a long, big drink off of the cold fresh beer in front of him.

"I came because I need your help," Morgy replied, tipping his beer back.

"Name it," Aidan replied. "What do you need?" He was intrigued. He knew that Morgy had more money than God himself, but he also wasn't one to miss an opportunity to help a friend in need. In fact, it was one of the few things that he still lived for.

"I've bought me a lot down in Texas along the gulf," he said, trying to suppress the smile on his face, but feeling it shining through his eyes nonetheless. Hurriedly, he took another drink so he wouldn't give himself away. He was a horrible liar. "...and I need someone to drive my bus down there while I follow in my truck."

Aidan knew that to an extent at least, he had already been bamboozled. Morgy had been trying to talk him into going *somewhere* and doing *something* ever since Dory had died. He had always managed to talk his way out of it though. Looking in Morgy's eyes for anything suspicious, he worked the thing around in his mind. It was, in the end, a legitimate favor and something that really needed doing. He would have to go along with it, even if it *was* a well orchestrated trick.

"When do you want to go?" Aidan asked.

"I'd like to go today," he replied. "But I can wait until tomorrow if that suits you better. We'll have to drive back to Illinois first and pick up the bus and then head south. The lot owner is a friend of mine from back home down there and he sort of jumped me ahead of a bunch of people for a prime spot when another old bastard died unexpectedly. I've got to get down there right away if I want the thing or he will have a full on retiree rebellion on his hands."

Aidan looked at his watch. There was still time to get to the bank before it closed, then go home and pack for the trip. "Damn it," he said. "Okay, let's go."

Morgy hurriedly drank down his beer and left a dollar on the bar.

"Put that in your pocket," Aidan said loudly. "We don't tip the God damned owner around here, only the hired help!"

"Hey!" The owner called out, reaching across the bar and grabbing the bill.

"Thanks Bill," Aidan said to the owner as they started for the door.

"Thank you, Gentlemen," Bill replied.

Morgy stopped for a second to admire the saying that hung over the bar "*Ilegitimus Non Carborundum,*" he read out loud. Morgy laughed. "That's Latin," he said. "Someone has a sense of humor around here at least."

"What's it mean?" Aidan asked as the door closed behind them.

"It means...," Morgy stopped for a second and lit a cigarette, "...don't let the bastards grind you down." Then he smiled at Aidan, knowing that he had done just that very thing.

"Good advice," Aidan said. "Now take me home so I can get some things. And don't let me forget to stop at the bank," he ordered.

Chapter 49   Anniversary Blues

Maizey couldn't remember anymore if it had been thirty or thirty-one years before when they had first been to Heroica Matamoros, México. Her and William had been visiting friends in Brownsville, Texas that year though, and had crossed the border to find some trinkets. They had gotten lost on a side street however in Heroica Matamoros, and ended up having one of the best times of their lives with the locals.

In the end, they had agreed to return the following year to stay an entire week during a fiesta and they had been returning every year since. Five years earlier, William had even surprised her, buying them an apartment of their own in the old neighborhood. It was the type of old Mexican neighborhood where most tourists would be afraid to venture, but for Maizey and William, it was like going home every year. They knew three and sometimes four generations of the families there who all knew them by name.

She had fretted and mulled over the decision of whether or not she should even go that year. She knew that William would want her to go and so many of the locals were expecting her. Especially the little ones for whom she always brought a bag full of gifts. But it wouldn't be the same since Bill had died shortly after returning from last year's trip.

She believed that it was actually brought on by something he had eaten down there. She was always warning him against patronizing the corner food vendors if he wasn't familiar with them. Still, he

217

almost never listened and every year he sought out new places and dishes. She was convinced that something had made him ill down there to cause him to get so sick so quickly. The doctors, however, called it pneumonia and ultimately, congestive heart failure. She supposed that it really didn't matter much either way though, because in the end it was his time and he had had one hell of a ride without many regrets.

It was hard for her at first. Hell, it was still hard being alone after so many years with the same man. Somewhere around twenty years or so, the other person starts to act as your own right arm and you begin to naturally assume that they will always be there as a part of yourself. It isn't until you lose them that you discover exactly how much you had come to depend upon them. It's only then that you discover just how hard you were actually leaning on the other person for your own support all along.

It wasn't even the obvious things that were the hardest. It never is. She figured out how to pay the bills in fairly short order. You opened them as they arrived and wrote the checks as you mailed them out. It was all pretty straight forward really. It was the simple stupid things that everyone should know how to do that turned out to be the most difficult for her. Like her dry cleaning for instance. Bill had always dropped it off and picked it up for her. She had no idea where to take it or how much it costs or what to even ask for. It was so stupid, but it was something she had just never had to do before. In the end it was things like that wore on her nerves almost every day.

It scared the hell out of her to think what sort of unforeseen obstacles she might encounter in Mexico, but she felt that it was something she had to do nonetheless, for their friends, for Bill, and for herself. She spent weeks trying to anticipate what to expect being on her own in Mexico, trying to remember what all it was that Bill used to do for her there. In the end she could only trust in her ability to get through whatever came at her.

It was 1980 and it would have been their forty-third wedding anniversary. Maizey was 64 years old and learning to be independent, really independent, for the first time in her life. Putting the last of her bags in the sedan, she returned to the house and checked the light switches each four more times. She checked the stove and the appliances and the light timers five times. She checked everything there was to check once more and felt for her car keys in her pocket. Then she turned and locked the door behind her. She was really doing it.

Turning away, she had a new found confidence that she hadn't known in years. She was sure of herself and walked out across the driveway with a certain jaunty stride. She was doing it, she *could* do it, and she really was *going* to do it. Starting the car, she checked her mirrors one more time as she slowly and carefully backed out of the drive, careful not to hit the mailbox...again.

Bill always joked about it, but she had hit that damned mailbox more times than she could even remember. He used to say that she was trying to kill the thing to stop her credit card bills from arriving so that he would never see the "evidence" of her latest crime against the household budget. She could ding the car all to hell and destroy a perfectly good mailbox, but Bill would just laugh it off and jump in the car to go and buy another one. He would graciously save the bulk of his jokes for later when her tears had stopped flowing. He was a good man and he had always taken good care of her. But now she was doing it all on her own.

"Damnit!" She screamed, and even over her engine and screeching brakes, the neighbor lady, Mrs. Thompson, heard her cursing and turned to look at her. "God damnit," she said again quietly, pulling the car back into the drive.

"You're really doing it alright," she said to herself as she parked the car again. She got out and walked to the door, unlocking the handle and then the deadbolt. Stepping inside, she reached down and picked up the white ball of warm fluff. "You thought I had forgotten you, didn't you?" she asked, but the cat only purred, thankful to be going along for the ride with her, wherever they might be going.

Somewhere in the distant reaches of the universe or some other alternative one, she heard Bill laughing. "You're really doing it," she imagined him saying, which only caused her to smile. "Now watch out for the mailbox," his voice came again inside her head and she hit the brakes just short of smashing into the thing again. Smiling even bigger now, she shook her head, cleared the mailbox and headed down the road toward old Mexico. Mrs. Thompson stood by the curb watching her all the while, wondering if she had finally lost her mind altogether.

Maizey gave her a friendly wave and drove on. Come hell or high water, or even a dead cat or two, by God, she really was doing it.

Chapter 50   Texas

Texas was exactly as Aidan had remembered it; a whole lot of hot and nothing much to look at. Pulling in to Palacios, Texas, he was surprised that it was their destination. It looked like a lot of other small towns in Texas with aging homes mixed with a spattering of trailers and several businesses with their windows boarded up. Aidan thought that living so close to the gulf must be a constant battle with the natural forces of wind, weather, and salty air to try to keep your home up and it looked like several of the locals were losing the war.

The hand painted signs on the local bar didn't seem to bode well for the tourist crowd much either and Aidan grumbled to himself as they passed it. If there was anything promising to the sensibilities of an Iowan yet, it was only the streets lined with short Texas palms. Aside from that, there were a dozen other places they had driven through on their way that would have been more appealing to him to stop and call home for a few weeks. Then they pulled in to the campsite.

Aidan had followed Morgy all the way, electing to drive the truck instead of "the bus," as Morgy called it. His "bus" was actually an almost forty foot long behemoth of a mobile home that he had purchased right before his wife died. Aidan never asked him, but he was certain that it must have cost ten times as much as Aidan had paid for his own modest home in Chariton.

Pulling into the drive of the park, Aidan had his breath taken away. Looking up and down the bay, he could see dozens of shrimp boats and countless small yachts and boats of every imaginable sort. The Tres Palacios Bay itself was a relatively calm body of the most beautiful, crystal clear blue waters that he had ever seen. Almost at the horizon, he could see the land mass that separated them from the Gulf of Mexico. Morgy pulled in to the vacant spot that looked directly across the bay. He could see now why Morgy had wanted to hurry to get it. It was incredible.

Either side of the camp spot was surrounded by mature trees so they could sit in the shade as of an evening and drink beer, talking about the fish they had caught and comparing stories with the neighbors. The entire grounds were full up with license plates on campers and RV's from almost every mid-west state. Aidan had never had much desire to be a 'snowbird' as they were called, but for the first time, he could at least begin to see the allure of it.

Morgy walked up beside him flashing the biggest shit-eating, prideful grin that he had ever recalled seeing him sport. "You can just pull the truck over there," he said, pointing to a nearby parking spot. "Nice, isn't it?" he asked as he turned away to begin permanently setting up the bus.

"Nice, hell," Aidan replied, "its God damned beautiful, bud."

They would spend the rest of the day setting up the bus and unloading the lawn furniture, followed by a trip in to town for groceries. For dinner, they treated themselves to fresh fried Gulf shrimp at the wood fronted Outrigger Restaurant. Aidan had never cared for fried shrimp, but these were unlike anything that he had ever tasted. There truly was nothing like them.

From his years of traveling with the railroad and driving trucks, he had learned to appreciate how strangers were usually treated decent in most places, but generally with little regard. In his youth, he had even liked that about traveling. After so many years of being frowned upon for who he was and where he had come from, he liked the anonymity. But he was older now, and more than anything, he had come to appreciate friendly faces, no matter where they reared their head. Just like the fried shrimp, the people he met first at the Outrigger, then all around Palacios, seemed to be the most genuinely friendly folks he had ever encountered anywhere. It wasn't that they were overly friendly, or simply being kind to a stranger either. Instead, they just had a way about them that put him at ease and made him want to stay and get to know them better.

That night, sitting in a lawn chair with Morgy and drinking a beer with a couple from Michigan while he looked out across the Bay and at the stars in the huge evening sky, Aidan could scarcely help but compare it to his time with MacGregor and Doran. There was something about sitting under the stars, drinking a beer, and being surrounded by friends that took him back to that time and place in his life and almost made him feel that he was somehow, albeit a thousand miles and half a century away, back home again.

The next morning, Morgy woke him even before he was ready. The cool, moist air floating through the window off of the Bay gave Aidan one of the best nights of sleep that he could remember in years. It was one of the first nights he could remember sleeping through without being awoken to the sound of men screaming and the smell of death and blood.

Aidan stepped out to Morgy handing him a fresh cup of black coffee. He had always liked the way Morgy made his coffee, the same way that he did, strong and thick and black. Very few people could drink either of their coffee, but in that regard, the two had always agreed. Looking back, it probably had something to do with their countless days together waiting for assignments in Europe. You had to stay awake and be ready at a moment's notice for an assignment that might not come in days or even weeks so the coffee was always on and it was always black as tar.

"What are we going to do today?" Aidan asked, taking a sip off the top of the burning hot cup.

"I have a surprise for you," Morgy replied, smiling. "How's the coffee?" he asked.

"Hot and black," he replied. "A surprise eh? It had better be dancin' girls then."

"Nope," Morgy replied, "even better. You're too damned old for dancing girls anyway."

Morgy pointed down toward the water. Tied to the little walkway that extended from their campsite into the water was a small fishing boat. Well, it was a big boat by Iowa standards, but it looked small compared to the rest of the boats around them.

"Did you rent us a boat from the Marina?" Aidan asked.

"Nope," Morgy replied. "I bought it. It's mine."

"You're pretty serious about this place, aren't you?" Aidan asked, taking another, larger sip off of his coffee.

"Serious as a heart attack," Morgy replied. "In fact, you may have to find another ride home."

"I'll just take your truck while you're out fishing," Aidan said, flashing a hint of a smile.

"No you won't," Morgy replied, throwing the rest of his coffee in to the coals from their fire pit, "because you are going with me. But, I will let you buy the bait."

"Deal," Aidan said. Whenever the two were together, Aidan was always working to make sure that he was paying his own way for everything. He knew that Morgy had tons of money, just like Morgy knew that Aidan didn't have much at all. So it was important to Aidan's pride for him to feel like he had paid his own way. To that end, Morgy stayed constantly on the lookout for little things here and there to have him pay for. It wasn't that he cared at all about it, but he knew that if he didn't let him pay for things here and there that he would find a wad of cash hidden somewhere in his bus six or eight months down the road.

Morgy couldn't have been more pleased with himself. He had done it. He had dragged Aidan out of the bar and got him to one of the handful of places on earth where a man can find himself again. There's something about the sunrise over the Bay and fishing in the Gulf that helps cure whatever ails a man's soul, Morgy had thought. And now that Aidan was here, all he needed to do was get him out on the water and let the water and the wind and the clear blue sky and sunshine work its magic on him. He had done it.

Chapter 51   Messed Up In Mexico

Maizey was glad that she had come. It was good to be back amongst their old friends. They had been very saddened to learn about Bill and all of them had taken special care to go out of their way for her as a result. The Mexican people that they had befriended were a wonderful lot. None of them had a terrible lot to give, but all of them gave of themselves what they could for a friend they perceived to be in need.

One of their oldest and closest friends, Marlina Vargas, came to call on her at their flat every morning, bringing with her tortillas and fresh ground coffee. Marlina was herself a widow and being about ten years older than Maizey she had always acted like her adopted big sister. Now that Maizey had lost her own husband, Marlina's doting had only intensified.

Maizey had been there for three weeks and it was time for her to be going home again. She had confided in Marlina how difficult the simple things had been for her, how she nearly forgot the cat and backed into the mailbox, and how she still wasn't sure how to order her prescription medications in three month increments the way Bill had always managed to get them. They were simple things, stupid really, but those were the things that seemed to stymie her at every turn.

Marlina though, had only smiled reassuringly and said, "The house does not rest upon the ground, but upon the woman. We are born to bear the weight of the world." Then, looking out the window thoughtfully she added, "the Lord God gives us only what we can take though."

Maizey got up and gave her old friend a hug. She promised that unlike when Bill had been alive, that she would spend more time there with her. "It's hard, but I'm not done living yet either, Marlina. And I'll be damned if I'm going to spend the rest of my life sitting at home doing nothing and waiting for death. I've seen too many friends end their lives that way, even my own mother."

"People born to be flower pots will never leave their porch," she said thoughtfully, "and you are no flower pot. Your place is in the field Maizey. You have always been a wild flower blowing in the wind, for as long as I have known you. Always."

"More like a Dutchman's Breeches," Maizey said laughing, "upside down mostly."

"Huh?" Marlina was confused by her friend's humor. She had always loved spending time with Maizey. She reminded her of a sister that she used to have, always smiling and so full of laughter and of life. Still, she never fully understood the things that she thought were funny. So she did what she always did to Maizey, she shrugged her shoulders, hugged her, and went on.

"Don't you worry Marlina," Maizey said, hugging her close before she headed on out the door, "I'm not going to let dry cleaning or cats or prescriptions stop me."

"Vaya Con Dias," Marlina said, smiling at her one last time before she turned and headed out the door.

"Good bye!" Maizey called after her, closing the door quietly behind her. "Oh damn. Prescriptions!" she said to herself, remembering that she had promised the neighbor back home that she would pick him up his heart medication. So many years of good, clean living only to be turned into a drug smuggler in her sixties. She giggled to herself at the thought of it.

While she still remembered, she wrote herself a note to go to the market and get the pills after she had finished packing. She then set the note on the table beside her car keys and placed a small agate on top as a weight. Bill had loved rocks, especially the shiny polished agates. He must have bought a thousand of them over the years. They were everywhere in her home and their Mexican flat too.

Turning away from the table, she stopped momentarily and thought. Then she turned back, picked up her pen and added to the note, "P.s. don't forget the damned cat!"

Chapter 52   Fresh Fish

Aidan took to life on the Bay. It was a place where each day seemed as fresh and clean and pure and perfect as the sunrise over the Gulf. There was something about the air and the water that cleansed your spirit each day anew. There had been times in his life when fishing had seemed like a chore, as if there was something else more important that he needed to be doing. But now, it relaxed him completely and cleared his mind of any worries. It was as if the ghosts dare not to disturb the peaceful solace of the water.

As the weeks wore on, Aidan spent more and more time on the small boat, just sitting, drinking beer, fishing, and soaking up the sun's rays. By the third week, Morgy had stopped going out with him altogether as Aidan would take the boat out in the morning at sunrise and not return until dark. It was too much for Morgy's back to sit out there for so long and secretly, he worried that Aidan might be using the boat as his new barstool, and nothing more. He had seen hope in the beginning, but with each day he worried more and more that his plan had ultimately failed to bring his old friend back from the land of the walking dead.

At the end of the third week Morgy decided that he would have to return home for a while to tend to some businesses there. He had never figured on being down here this long and there were some matters at home that would wait no more. He offered however, for Aidan to stay behind and fish if he wanted. Aidan accepted the offer, saying that he would like to stay for another couple of weeks before going home. He might even come back after taking care of some things himself, he confided, and buy a camper and boat to call his own.

"I'll leave in a couple of days," Morgy had said that evening. "But first I'd like to make a run down to Old Mexico. Have you ever been?"

"No. I never made it this far south before," Aidan replied.

"You should come with me then. It will do you good to take a day off from the boat. I'm worried that you're going to get sun cancer sitting out there all the time," he joked. "And besides, doesn't that bother your back?"

"Are you kidding? My joints haven't felt this good in years," Aidan replied. "I didn't even know how much they hurt all the time until I came here and everything quit hurting. I mean, shit, I don't even want to go back home, it feels so good."

"Great! See, I told you that you'd love it down here," Morgy said smiling and giving his friend a little wink. "You want to go to Mexico with me tomorrow then? I promised my sister I would pick her up a few things."

Morgy had been sitting in a lawn chair beside the small fire. Aidan stood drinking a beer across from him and looked down at his friend's expectant eyes. He really had no desire to go to Old Mexico or anywhere else for that matter. He was content to just spend his days alone, drinking beer out on the gulf and fishing for his dinner.

When he was a kid, he and Doran had hunted for their dinners a thousand times. It was work and desperation and disappointment and hunger. But now, here, it was something altogether different. There was something so natural and fulfilling about eating what you had provided for yourself. He had the money to buy whatever he wanted from wherever he wanted to go, but nothing was as pure and good as what he had caught for himself. It just tasted better than anything else.

Aidan had thought a lot about that lately sitting out in the boat alone. He had remembered how hard the bad times had been, and how good they had been as well. There were a lot of people that he missed these days that had gone before him. He only wished that they could all be there with him now to enjoy the taste of the fresh, plentiful meals that the water provided.

"I remember the good old days," one of the snow bird neighbors had said as a dozen or so of them had converged upon Morgy and Aidan's camp fire one evening, "when a loaf of bread only cost a dime. Now you go to the store and a loaf of bread is liable to cost you over two dollars!"

"Yeah," Aidan had replied squinting his eye at the man who in Aidan's opinion, talked entirely too much, "well I've got the money now to buy as much bread as I want, but who in the hell had an extra dime back then?"

The entire campfire had burst into laughter at the remark, and even the man who talked too much had to laugh and nod his head in agreement.

Aidan turned his attention back to Morgy who still sat waiting for an answer to the lingering question on Old Mexico. Of course Aidan didn't want to go. He had absolutely no desire to leave this place or do anything or go anywhere, let alone Mexico. He had never met a Mexican that he needed to meet again in his opinion, so why bother going to see a whole damned country full of them? But in the end, he could tell that Morgy wanted him to go along.

"Yeah, sure, Bud," Aidan said. "I've never been to Mexico. That sounds great." He was lying of course. It sounded simply awful and miserable. But he could see by the smile on Morgy's face and the twinkle in his eyes that he had genuinely wanted him to go and his agreement made his old friend very happy. And in the end what else is there in life, but taking every opportunity to make your few remaining old friends happy? For Aidan, there was nothing else really.

Chapter 53   God Blessed Shale

The Mexican border town market district was a virtual sea of grey and balding heads moving along the walkway lined streets. Morgy seemed very excited by the shops and the people, but Aidan found it dizzying. He had never liked crowds, or crowded places. In fact, throughout his entire life, he had worked to avoid even going to the grocery store unless it was late at night or early in the morning.

The main street leading into Heroica Matamoros in Mexico was nothing like Aidan had expected. The fresh pavement of the main thoroughfare glistened in the early afternoon sun. The road was divided by medians adorned with well kept landscaping and trimmed trees. Running along the busier four-lane street were other well manicured medians separating single lanes on either side for local, slower moving traffic. It was one of the more well thought out, better maintained, and safer city street designs that he had ever seen. It could have been in the wealthy suburbs of an American city, but he'd never thought of Mexico as being so modern or the people being so ingenious.

Morgy had wanted to visit a stretch of shops that he had been to before and surprise his sister with a painting from an artist that she had admired during a previous trip. But Aidan had never been much taken by paintings or art. He preferred the beauty of the natural world any day of the week. How could you paint a picture or snap a photo and really understand what it felt like to be sitting in the Gulf as the sun rose before you? It was in his mind, an incredible waste of time on the part of the artist, and an equally incredible waste of money for those who bought the stuff.

Driving off the main road, Aidan had noticed a fishing tackle store and opted to walk back to it while Morgy shopped for his art. As Aidan walked, he found the sidewalk to be busier and busier with the slow moving sea of grey hairs weaving in and out in front of him. Not only did it make him dizzy as he was still tall enough to look out across the tops of most of their heads, but it also rather annoyed him.

He was getting older himself these days and he might even be older than half the crowd, but that didn't mean that he had to act like they did. They were old and slow and hunched over. They wore pants around their chests. His body ached more than most, he reckoned, but still, despite his pain and its natural tendency to want to fold over upon itself, he stood tall and walked proudly. It was his way and no amount of age would ever change *that*.

What's more, old people in groups had a tendency to stop for no reason at all and just stand there. It was as if they didn't get the concept of staying to the right while you walked just like you did when you were driving. Worse still, none of them got the concept of moving the hell out of the way for faster moving walkers no matter which side of the walk they were on. It was more than he could take. The three blocks was beginning to seem like an eternity. Finally he stepped off the sidewalk and began to walk down the edge of the road, looking back into the slow moving, aimless sea of old tourists with contempt.

Aidan looked on at the lethargic mass of heads and faces, sometimes making eye contact with them as they passed, but usually simply viewing them as a whole, rather than a collection of individuals. It was then that he felt it. The familiar click in his step, and stopping, he lifted his foot behind him to reveal that sure enough, even here on the clean, well paved streets a thousand miles from home, his shoe had picked up an unwelcome straggler.

"What in the hell?", he said to himself aloud, already annoyed by circumstance, but now moved to near utter madness at the sight of a chunk of razor sharp shale stuck in the rubber of his shoe. "You've got to be kidding me. God damned shale!" He said, pulling the rock chip from his shoe and tossing it toward the median in the road. It was proof positive that the curses of his life, both great and small, would continue to follow him to the ends of the earth.

Chapter 54   A Curse to Remember

It was very busy in town that day, and Maizey had to park her car several blocks away to get anywhere near the pharmacy she favored. The little shop had been there since they had started coming to Heroica Matamoros and the shopkeeper had become a friend of Bill's before he had passed. They even had gone fishing together on a number of occasions in his last years. It was a bit out of her way really and took longer to get to than the neighborhood pharmacies near their flat, but they had always believed in being loyal customers that way. And it would give her an opportunity to share the news of the passing of her husband with one of his old friends.

She knew that she had quite a walk ahead of her and the streets were particularly busy with snowbirds that day. So, while in no particular urgent hurry, she had opted to walk along the outside edge of the sidewalk. She loved the crowds though and exchanged pleasant greetings with anyone who would exchange a glance. It was just her way. She had always believed that kindness to strangers had a way of perpetuating itself into creating a better world and this day was no exception. Besides, she was at a place in her life where there was no need to be in a rush again, ever.

It was there, walking along that she saw him; the tall, older man walking out in the road. She knew that he must be new to the area or he would never chance to walk out in the street. The local cab drivers were as fast and dangerous as any big city American cabbies. But here especially, they had a way of whipping in off the main thoroughfare and screeching to a halt along the business lane. No one in their right mind who had ever seen them drive would walk out there on purpose and she thought momentarily about issuing the man a word of warning.

As she neared him they exchanged eye contact and she began to form the words to speak to him about the peril his life was in. As she did so he began to curse at his shoe of all things and she knew that he must have lost his mind. Niceties aside, she was not about to converse with a crazy old man on the streets of Mexico and decided it best that she leave him be. The Lord, she believed, took special care to look out for such people and she walked on by him. Despite her former concern for him, she tried not to make further eye contact while he cursed and threw something into the road toward the passing cars.

As she passed the crazy man though, she heard him cursing. "God damned shale," he said, and the voice stopped her in her tracks. Standing there, the crowd moved slowly around her as she wondered over the seeming familiarity of the stranger's voice. She *knew* that voice from somewhere, but where? With a furrowed brow, she searched her memory for where she had heard that voice before. Was it someone they had met in Mexico? Or perhaps an old friend of Bill's from Ohio? What about Melrose?

Suddenly Maizey felt her heart sink deep into her stomach. In an instant her eyes filled with moisture, and she swallowed hard to clear her throat. Turning around, she saw the man slowly ambling away down the street away from her, and she called to him from behind, "Aidan?"

Hearing his name from the crowd behind him, Aidan stopped and turned back. It was an unfamiliar woman's voice and he was certain that it was probably some woman calling for her husband of the same name. Instead, he saw a woman walking slowly toward him with her mouth agape and looking almost scared as she neared him.

Only feet away, but still standing on the sidewalk the old woman looked at him. She was about his age, he reckoned, and with the stout build of a country woman accustomed to working hard and eating well. There was a kind softness in her face that even the wrinkles couldn't hide and she had the most beautiful green eyes with drops of... "Oh my God," he said quietly, almost to himself, "twice as much in the left. It's you."

Slowly, as if led by some strange gravity that drew them nearer one another, their feet shuffled forward. At first, they acted as if they were merely old friends exchanging polite and simple greetings. The entire thing seemed surreal, a thousand miles and decades had passed only to find them standing there staring into one another's eyes once more surrounded by hundreds of passing strangers. Still, their souls led them closer and before even they knew what was happening, they stood, embracing one another, tears streaming down their aged faces, in a street in a border town in Old Mexico.

Chapter 55   Fin

The year was 1981 when Aidan and Maizey had finally found one another, 48 years after she stood alongside the road waiting for him. In a lot of ways that even she had never fully understood or accepted, she had always been waiting for him.

The two would spend the next twenty years inseparably bouncing between Ohio and South Texas where Aidan would purchase a boat and a "bus" of their own. Then they'd hop on down to Old Mexico to spend part of their winter with Maizey's old friends. Not very often, but sometimes, every once in a while, they would get in their car too, and make the long drive home, placing flowers on the graves of the ghosts of Melrose.

Aidan still visited with the ghosts, all of them at different times. But when they spoke, they did so on his terms those days, when he felt the time was right and simply wanted to talk with them. Likewise, he still awoke at times to the smell of death and the screams of the men, but they too would subside and quickly fade as he would turn in his bed to find Maizey sleeping soundly beside him.

He almost never felt the need to drink after that either. He did so sometimes anyways, like whenever Morgy would stop down to visit them he would always join him in a beer or two. But Aidan found the sweet intoxication of the Gulf to be enough. Well, that and the feeling he always got whenever he looked into those eyes; those eyes...looking back at him with their tiny drops of chocolate, the left one with twice as much as the right; twice as much. They warmed his heart and moved his soul to tears. Until the day he died, he could look into those eyes and feel himself melt. Like the stars under a clear country sky, or a sunrise over the Gulf, those eyes...they took his breath away, every time, always. *Always.*

In 2003, after twenty-two wonderful years together, Aidan died at the age of 87. He died peacefully, diagnosed with terminal cancer one day, and dead less than a week later. The very last thing he did in this world was look into Maizey's eyes and whisper, "I love you," and for the final time, she took his breath away. They say that the edges of his lips seemed to curl upwards as he exhaled, as if in a smile.

As per his wishes, he was buried in a small cemetery not far from Melrose. Maizey was surprised at the turnout of people there. There were flowers and cards as if he had been thirty years younger and never left the area.

Later, amongst the cards she found a handwritten letter, and this is what it said:

Dear Maizey;

I did not well know the man you knew as Aidan, for we always called him by another nickname around these parts. But in the end no matter what you called him, I was only happy to be able to call him my friend.

His story, that which I knew of it, was a long and sad one filled with heartache and sorrow. His was one of the saddest stories I have ever known. However, it is also one with the happiest ending of any I have ever witnessed. He told me once that he would go through it all again a hundred times over to only end up with you only once. Thank you for giving my friend, and his story, a happy ending. And thank you for bringing him home to us to rest.

Sincerely,
A Son of Melrose

Today, Maizey is in her nineties. She doesn't get to Mexico any more, or Texas. In fact, she even ended up selling her home in Ohio. She lives with her younger brother and his wife not far from where it all began, in a little Southern Iowa town that is close enough to the big city to visit the stores and casinos, but not too far from Melrose to visit and walk along the roads and put flowers on the graves.

So next time you're passing through the town on your way to the lake, slow down if you happen to see an old woman there. If you get a close enough look you may even notice the tiny drops of chocolate in her sparkling green eyes. At first glance she'll seem to be all alone in the desolate remains of the dying town. But if you ask her, she'll tell you that there, all around you are a thousand lives and stories. And she can tell you too that smiling at you from almost every direction...are the ghosts of Melrose. *Always.*

Dear Reader;

Thank you for reading *The Ghosts of Melrose*. I would love to hear your thoughts and comments about the book. To contact me or to see what I am up to next, please visit my web site: www.buzzmalone.com

As an independent writer without a big New York City agent or publishing house, my success or failure depends upon you. If you enjoyed this book, please tell your friends about it and visit Amazon.com to leave a positive review of the book.

Buzz Malone